P9-CQR-510

A FLAWLESS KISS

Sarah was lost in thought when Lord Chance abruptly reached out to grasp her arm. Coming to a halt, Sarah glanced up at his handsome countenance in surprise.

"What is it?"

His dark gaze moved over her pale features, lingering a heart-stopping moment on her lips before seeking her wide eyes.

"I said when we first met you were extraordinary. I did not fully comprehend just how extraordinary."

"Ridiculous. I am no way out of the common— unless you consider the fact that I am the daughter of the Devilish Dandy."

"You are Miss Sarah Cresswell, and never have I encountered a woman who would behave such as you."

She gave a breathy laugh. "Now that I readily believe."

Without warning, his hands reached up to cup her face. "I would admire them more if they did."

Her heart again gave that disturbing lurch and, barely aware she was moving, she leaned toward the heat of his body. She might be all that was sensible, but a force beyond her control held her spellbound as his dark head lowered and he claimed her mouth in a demanding kiss. . . .

Books by Debbie Raleigh

LORD CARLTON'S COURTSHIP

LORD MUMFORD'S MINX

A BRIDE FOR LORD CHALLMOND

A BRIDE FOR LORD WICKTON

A BRIDE FOR LORD BRASLEIGH

THE CHRISTMAS WISH

Published by Zebra Books

THE
CHRISTMAS
WISH

Debbie Raleigh

ZEBRA BOOKS
Kensington Publishing Corp.
http://www.zebrabooks.com

ZEBRA BOOKS are published by

Kensington Publishing Corp.
850 Third Avenue
New York, NY 10022

All Kensington titles, imprints and distributed lines are available at special quantity discounts for bulk purchases for sales promotion, premiums, fund-raising, educational or institutional use.

Special book excerpts or customized printings can also be created to fit specific needs. For details, write or phone the office of the Kensington Special Sales Manager: Kensington Publishing Corp., 850 Third Avenue, New York, NY 10022. Attn. Special Sales Department. Phone: 1-800-221-2647.

Zebra and the Z logo Reg. U.S. Pat. & TM Off.

First Printing: November 2001
10 9 8 7 6 5 4 3 2 1

Printed in the United States of America

One

As was his habit, Oliver Spense, Earl of Chance, was happily ensconced in his library with a large crate recently arrived from Greece. Perhaps few of his cronies would have contemplated the latest delivery of broken pottery and priceless statues with such reverence, but it was well known that while the Flawless Earl was unparalleled upon the sporting field, a master on the dance floor, and a demon at the card table, he did possess the oddest fancy for dusty relics. His peculiar tendency was happily overlooked, not only because it did one's social position great credit to be numbered among his friends, but also because he possessed the good sense not to burden his acquaintances with tedious details of his studies.

Chance, a tall, well-muscled gentleman with dark hair and piercing black eyes, was supremely indifferent to others' opinions of his fascination with the ancient world. Indeed, he was rarely bothered with others' opinions of himself in general. It was not so much arrogance as a deep contentment with his well-ordered life.

This morning, he was particularly content. A rare smile lightened his strong features and lessened his rather imposing air. With exquisite care, he lifted the fragile shard of pottery to better view it in the pale November sunlight that tumbled into the room. Soon he would set it aside so he could sketch its likeness onto a pad, but for the moment he was lost in the thoughts of citizens traversing the streets of ancient Athens.

The pleasant imaginings occupied his attention for several minutes. Then the quite unexpected sound of the library door being thrust open cast his thoughts to the wind. Slowly raising his head, he silently watched the small, nearly bald servant cross the vast room.

Chance allowed his smile to fade, although no hint of annoyance at the intrusion could be detected on his sternly handsome features. He had discovered long ago that a soft-spoken, impassive demeanor was far more daunting than any number of rages. Indeed, he had become so skilled that only the bravest or the most foolish dared to cross his considerable will.

Leaning back in his wing chair, Chance templed his slender fingers beneath his blunt chin.

The butler halted and offered a stiff bow. "Pardon me, my lord."

"I fear you mistook the time, Pate," Chance offered in gracious tones.

The butler, who had been with Chance since his arrival in London ten years before, was one of the rare few who did not panic beneath that unwavering black gaze. "No, my lord. It is precisely half past ten."

"And at half past ten do I care to be interrupted?"

"No, my lord," Pate conceded with a faint hint of regret. "You have been very specific that you are not to be disturbed between the hours of eight and eleven.''

Certainly not an unreasonable gentleman, Chance did possess a handful of eccentricities he expected his staff to honor. He forbade any sort of puddings to be placed upon his table, insisted his hounds be accorded the utmost care, and demanded his mornings be dedicated solely to his studies. Hardly arduous requests, he told himself, considering the outrageous habits of many noblemen.

Now he regarded his servant with the mildest hint of reproof.

"And yet here you are at precisely half past ten."

The butler's wooden countenance betrayed no emotion at the chastisement. "Yes, my lord."

"Perhaps the house is on fire?"

"No."

"Have the French invaded?"

The faintest hint of a twinkle entered Pate's faded blue eyes. "Not to my knowledge, my lord."

"Then I can only presume the Prince Regent has chosen this ungodly hour to call."

"Not the prince, but Mr. Coltran."

A hint of surprise flickered over Chance's handsome features. Although his younger brother often called at the elegant town house, more often than not when he was on the dun, he had never before dared to impose himself during Chance's studies.

"Good lord, is he foxed?" Chance drawled.

"I do not believe so."

"Odd. I never thought Ben to be particularly

stupid. Impetuous, ill advised, and reckless, certainly, but not stupid."

"He did say it was of the utmost urgency, my lord."

Chance allowed a faint smile to touch his lips. He was not bothered by his servant's pleas for leniency for Ben. His younger brother was an engaging scamp with more charm than sense. Few could fail to find a place in their heart for the spirited youth, himself included, but over the past several months his affections had been strained to the very limit.

"Yes, I daresay," Chance agreed, with a heroic effort at patience. "Everything is of the utmost urgency with my younger brother. His temperament is unfortunately rash, which no doubt accounts for his shocking lack of skill at the card table and his presence in my foyer."

"Yes, sir."

Allowing his hands to drop, Chance absently drummed his fingers on the arms of his chair. A small silence descended within the decidedly masculine room with its towering bookcases and solid mahogany furnishings.

"I suppose you believe I should see him despite my firm insistence at not being pestered by servants, visitors, and relatives on the dun?"

Pate gave a small cough. "He does appear quite undone."

Chance heaved a well-earned sigh. "And I would be a villain to force the charming rascal to extricate himself from troubles of his own making?"

"As you say."

"Oh, very well." Chance waved a pale hand. "If I do not see him, he will no doubt flee to

Mother, who will then arrive to complain of my gruesome lack of sensibilities for my poor sibling."

"Very good." Bowing deftly, the servant backed out of the room, leaving Chance to his thoughts.

At moments such as this, he missed his father the most. Although he had been one and twenty and out of the house when the previous earl had succumbed to an infection of the lungs, his brother had been only eleven. The loss had struck the young boy deeply, and Lady Chance had quite naturally spoiled him shamelessly. As a result, Ben's high spirits and reckless lack of responsibility had gone unchecked. Such a combination was destined to create disaster when he arrived in London. Within a month, he had lost his allowance at the card tables. He had also spent a great deal more on lavish extravagances and openhanded generosity toward any scoundrel with a sad tale.

In the beginning, Chance was forgiving when Ben turned to him for assistance. Most young bucks kicked up their heels upon their arrival in town. While he had personally never found enjoyment in drunken larks or gaming hells, he had been hopeful that such pastimes would soon pale on Ben.

Unfortunately, his hopes had been sorely dashed. Far from growing weary of his fast play, Ben had acquired a group of fribbles who had urged him into outlandish behavior that Chance would not tolerate. On the last occasion he had paid his brother's debts, he had sternly warned he would endure no more. He had demanded Ben mend his scandalous behavior or risk being removed to the country.

Clearly the threat had fallen upon deaf ears, Chance acknowledged with a flare of annoyance. Perhaps he should have the unruly scamp sent back to Kent. A few months of rusticating might return his sadly lacking wits.

With that firm thought in mind, Chance watched his younger sibling enter the room. His resolve was momentarily undermined at the sight of Ben. As Pate had claimed, he did look quite undone. His clothes appeared to have been slept in, his dark locks were tangled, and there was a visible paleness to his boyish features. Most disturbing of all was the absence of his ready smile, which had made him a favorite among all who met him.

Chance felt a faint qualm before his determination returned. One day his brother's impetuous nature would land him in trouble not even Chance's considerable power would be able to save him from. He intended to halt his foolishness without further delay.

Striding directly to the desk, Ben shoved an unsteady hand through his curls. "Chance, thank God you are at home."

"Since I am always at home at this particular time there was no need for any heavenly intervention."

Ben grimaced at the pointed words. "Oh, yes . . . I suppose you are angry I intruded upon your studies."

"Not as angry as I shall no doubt become once you have confessed your latest scrape," Chance retorted. "You might as well have a seat."

Ben gave a cursory glance toward the leather chair, but rather than sitting, he tugged at his cravat, a sure sign he was deeply in the bumble broth.

"You make this devilish difficult, you know," he complained.

"Me?" Chance lifted his dark brows. "As I recall, I have done nothing more sinister than allow you to intrude upon a perfectly lovely day."

"If you weren't so damned perfect upon all occasions, I shouldn't feel such a heel coming to you," Ben charged.

"How wretchedly inconvenient of me," Chance drawled. "Shall I lose the family fortune upon the turn of a card? Or do you prefer I have myself hauled before the magistrate for tipping over the watch?"

Ben favored him with a sour frown. "You could at least have the decency to have caused one scandal. It is deuced difficult to speak with a gentleman who has never so much as raised a brow among Society."

"Egad, how dreary I sound."

"Well, one would think so, considering the time you spend with those musty relics." Ben wrinkled his nose as he glanced toward the statue on the table. "But somehow you still manage to be the toast of London. You cannot conceive how tedious it is to be forever informed of your superior position or to have every maiden in town approaching me in hopes of acquiring an introduction to the Flawless Earl. Why, even my own friends flounder for hours attempting to ape your style with a cravat."

Although many gentlemen might have preened secretly beneath such fulsome flattery, Chance merely narrowed his gaze. "Good lord, it must be even worse than I feared," he pronounced.

"You can save such nonsense for your twitty friends. What has occurred?"

The tug on the cravat became more pronounced, causing Chance to worry the young man might actually strangle himself.

"I . . . I fear I have outspent my allowance."

Chance's expression did not waver. "There is nothing astonishing in that—although I do not precisely comprehend what has led you to fall upon my charity," he said softly. "On the last occasion you applied to me for a loan, I quite clearly warned you I would not be held responsible for any more of your debts. Did you misunderstand me?"

A dull flush stained Ben's youthful features before draining away to leave him even more pale than before.

"No, which is precisely why I am in such a bloody mess."

Chance experienced a flare of exasperation at his bother's petulant tone. He sounded more a child of five than a grown man. "I can hardly be blamed for your thorough lack of sense," he mocked. "What have you done? Gone to see the vultures?"

"I wish to God I had," Ben retorted fiercely.

The quaver in his brother's voice made Chance pause. What the deuce could the boy have been up to? "You had best tell me what is wrong."

Forgoing his maltreated cravat, Ben lifted his hands to scrub them over his face. "It is not easy to explain."

"Ben, I am swiftly losing what little patience I possess."

The very softness of his tone forced Ben to reluctantly lift his head and meet Chance's black gaze. "Very well." He swallowed heavily. "I said I had outrun my allowance, and since you had been so devilish disobliging as to refuse me another groat, I was forced to go elsewhere."

"Where did you go?"

There was a highly dramatic pause. "Lord Maxwell."

Chance drew in a sharp breath. Gads, this was a complication he had not expected. *And why should I,* a dark voice responded. Lord Maxwell's reputation for ruthlessly fleecing the gullible and desperate was renowned throughout London. It had never occurred to him Ben would be so birdwitted as to seek out the devil.

Chance leaned slowly forward. "Have you taken leave of you senses? Only the worst sort of greenhorn would place himself in the power of that blackguard."

A stubborn defiance descended upon Ben's countenance. "Well, I hadn't much choice unless I wished to be hauled to Newgate. Unfortunately, Maxwell refused to loan me money unless I provided him with a symbol of good faith."

A distinct sense of dread was beginning to lodge itself in Chance's stomach. "And what symbol did he request?"

"The Chance diamonds."

With a slow, lethal motion, Chance rose to his feet, his expression causing Ben to take a hasty step backward. "You did not hand over the family jewels to that scoundrel." It was more a statement than a question.

"N-no," Ben stuttered, clearly wishing he were anywhere but standing before his brother. "I did not have the opportunity."

"Explain."

"I . . . I went to Mother's and borrowed her jewels . . ."

"Borrowed?" Chance leaned forward, placing his hands flat on the desk. "You mean you stole them."

"It was only until my allowance arrived and I could repay the loan."

Chance ground his teeth. Good gads, the boy was beyond foolish. To think he would steal from his own mother . . .

"You do not believe for a moment Maxwell would have returned the jewels," he charged in low tones. "You fool, he would have claimed you sold them to him, and not a soul could have proved otherwise."

It was obvious the thought had never entered his thick skull. Ben gave a startled blink.

"As I said, I did not give them to him," Ben stammered. "I put them in the safe intending to give them to him, but when I awoke this morning I discovered they were gone."

Chance abruptly straightened. "Gone?"

"Someone has stolen them."

The town house in the modest neighborhood of London looked much like any other. Narrow, with a bow window and tidy garden, it hardly fit the image of the setting for the daughter of the most notorious thief in London.

But then, what had he expected? Chance asked himself.

Certainly something more in keeping with the flamboyance of the Devilish Dandy, a tiny voice answered. After all, few throughout London were not acquainted with the rumors surrounding the near legendary gentleman. A charming, intelligent master of disguise, he had freely moved through the continent and England, stealing only the rarest jewelry and works of art before disappearing into obscurity. Indeed, it became almost fashionable to have lost one's most precious heirlooms to the famous criminal, and more than one hostess had been known to complain bitterly at the end of her party that her gathering clearly had not been of high enough standards to garner the attention of the Devilish Dandy.

His sparkling career had come to a sharp end several months before, when he had been ratted out by one of his cohorts. He had been hauled to Newgate and awaited his fate with the noose, only to slyly slip away from beneath the very noses of the guards. It was commonly believed he had fled to India to escape the Crown's determination to have him dangling by the neck.

He had left behind three daughters, one of whom Lord Scott had promised Chance was the perfect solution to his current difficulties. Chance was far less certain. Although he placed the utmost confidence in his good friend, he had far less confidence in the daughter of a common thief. Good gads, would he be any less of a nitwit than Ben to trust such a woman?

Despite his hesitation, however, Chance had found himself standing before the narrow house just three days after the theft of the jewels. Not because he had suddenly discovered a desire to mix company with scoundrels, but because quite simply he hadn't the least notion of how to begin his search.

With a faint sigh at his own foolishness, Chance forced his well-shod feet to carry him to the front door. He could hardly stand in the street all day, he told himself. Still, with reluctance he lifted the knocker and gave it a sharp rap.

He was left standing for only a moment before the door was pulled open to reveal a short, square man with a face that had seen its share of battles. Chance felt a flare of surprise as he recognized the man as a boxer who had retired several years before. He had seen him in action on only two occasions, but there was no mistaking the wide, flattened nose, the cold blue eyes, and the missing front tooth.

"Yes?" the distinctly odd butler demanded with a suspicious glare.

"I am here to see Miss Cresswell." Chance held out a gold-edged salver. "My card."

The butler carefully studied the card before nodding his head and stepping backward.

"Aye, she be expecting you." As Chance entered the cramped foyer, the one-time boxer accepted the earl's caped driving coat and hat, then stalked up the stairs. Chance was forced to scurry to keep pace and nearly stumbled over the servant when the boxer stopped to push open a door and stick his head inside. "The gent's here."

"Thank you, Watts," a soft, wholly female voice answered from within.

Stepping aside, Watts carefully watched as Chance stepped past his solid form. As for Chance, he was no less suspicious. Although he could give himself a reasonable accounting at Jackson's, he was certainly no match for a genuine bruiser, even one closer to fifty than forty. And of course, being alone in such a household was hardly conducive to setting him at ease.

Not that there was anything particularly menacing in the surroundings, he was forced to concede. The room was rather plain, with a handful of delicate furnishings and satinwood paneling. He spotted one respectable landscape and a vase that might have been from the Ming Dynasty, but there was certainly nothing opulent or excessively vulgar. In fact, it was tastefully modest.

Assured he was not about to be besieged by a gang of ruffians, Chance slowly turned to regard the eldest daughter of the Devilish Dandy standing in the center of the room.

And promptly froze in astonishment.

Good gads, there had to be some mistake.

Standing before him, a tall woman with strong features and thick chestnut curls regarded him with steady blue eyes. Though she was attired in a trim rose gown, he might have suspected she was just another servant if not for the brilliant sapphire which hung from a delicate gold chain about her slender neck.

This was Sarah Cresswell?

This was the daughter of the Devilish Dandy?

As he gawked like the veriest moonling, the growling voice of the butler abruptly intruded into his disjointed thoughts.

"You have only to call if you need me, miss," he warned, with a pointed glare toward the silent Chance.

"Of course."

There was a short silence as Watts backed from the room, careful to leave the door open as if expecting to need to rush to the aid of his employer at any moment.

Chance gave a slow shake of his head. No one was less likely to need aid than this annoyingly calm maiden. She looked for all the world as if she received visits from titled gentlemen every day of the week. And perhaps she did, he wryly reassured himself, although she hardly looked the part. Unlike him, there were always gentlemen who preferred mistresses who pretended to be modest and virtuous females.

At last she offered a faint smile. "Welcome, my lord. Can I offer you anything? I have brandy which I am told is particularly fine."

Attempting to gather his usual composure, Chance narrowed his gaze. "You are Miss Cresswell?"

"Yes. You seem surprised," she retorted.

"Frankly, I am."

A distinct twinkle entered her eyes, forcing Chance to acknowledge she was a remarkably handsome woman despite her ill-reputed connections, a thought that in no way pleased him.

"You were expecting me to possess horns and a tail?"

His handsome features were sternly smoothed into unreadable lines. It was time to gain command of the situation. "I was not expecting a governess," he retorted with a soft thrust.

Her calm never wavered. "I assure you I have never been a governess. Please, will you have a seat?"

Chance hesitated, debating whether to simply walk out. Then, shrugging, he moved to settle himself in a brocade chair. For Lord Scott's sake, he would at least be polite.

He waited with commendable patience as his hostess moved to the sideboard to pour him a measure of brandy and did not even flinch when she unexpectedly stumbled and brushed against him, nearly dumping the drink down the front of his elegant moss green jacket. She was swift to right herself and place the glass safely in his hand.

"Thank you," he murmured.

Taking a seat across from him, Miss Cresswell regarded him with that peculiar stillness. "Lord Scott tells me that you have lost a diamond necklace and tiara."

Chance allowed the faintest hint of a mocking smile to curve his lips. "I am thankfully not in the habit of losing irreplaceable heirlooms. My brother, however, has foolishly allowed them to be stolen."

"Yes, that was foolish," she mocked in return. "I believe the jewelry belonged to Lady Chance."

A reluctant prick of interest stirred deep within Chance. It was not often a woman managed to surprise him. "Yes."

"Your wife?"

"My mother." He set aside the brandy as he recalled himself to the unpleasant matter at hand. "She has not yet learned they are missing."

"She must possess a great number of jewels not to have noticed a missing diamond necklace and tiara."

"This particular set is priceless and rarely removed from the safe. Of course, the one occasion when it is removed is during my mother's annual Yuletide Ball."

She studied him for a silent moment. "Why have you not told her the truth?"

"Because she labors beneath the mistaken belief that her youngest son is without fault. I do not wish to have her discover he is an irresponsible cad."

"She is bound to realize what has occurred. Christmas is only a month away."

"Not if I discover the jewels before Christmas."

"Which is what you desire from me."

Chance gave a small shrug. "Lord Scott convinced me you possessed certain skills that would be useful in my search. Unfortunately, I do not believe you would be at all suitable."

His soft words did nothing more than to cause her arched brows to slowly lift. "You have made that decision after such a brief meeting?"

"Yes."

"May I inquire why?"

"Because I presumed that you would be . . ." He forced himself to be as delicate as possible. "Older and far more experienced."

"I fail to comprehend what my age has to do with the situation." She deliberately misinterpreted his words.

Chance pressed his lips together. It would serve her right if he informed her he had been expecting a brazen doxy who consorted with the dregs of Society. Instead, he lifted an elegant shoulder. "Because this might very well prove to be dangerous."

"Then you shall certainly be in need of my help," she informed him in firm tones.

Chance gave a blink at her audacity. He had to admit he had never before encountered a female quite like Miss Cresswell. "You believe you are more capable of overcoming danger than myself?"

"Of course."

"Absurd."

Her astonishingly blue eyes narrowed. "Do you realize, Lord Chance, that you possess an alarming tendency to believe what people wish you to believe?"

Why, the saucy wench. Chance was uncertain whether to laugh or slay her with a few blighting words.

"If you wish to imply I am easily fooled, Miss Cresswell, then I fear you are wide of the mark," he replied in dangerous tones. "I have yet to be culled by even the most cunning scoundrel."

"Indeed." The sparkle in her blue eyes deepened as she slowly lifted a slender hand to reveal a stickpin with a particularly fine diamond. "I believe this is yours, sir."

Thoroughly disarmed, Chance regarded his property in disbelief. The chit must have stolen it when she had so awkwardly handed him his brandy, although with such skill he had not even suspected her devious intent—and after he had promised himself he would be firmly on his guard.

For one of the few times in his life, Chance found himself thoroughly unnerved. "Good God, Miss Cresswell, do you make a habit of stealing other people's property?" he demanded in tight tones.

She remained supremely unrepentant. "I merely wished to prove a point."

"And what point is that?"

"That being an arrogant, condescending earl might ensure your success among Society, but it will serve you little in tracking down a thief," she said smoothly. "If you truly desire the return of the diamonds, then you will swallow your pride and admit you are in need of my help."

For a moment a flare of outrage raced through

his body at her blunt insult. No one spoke to
the Earl of Chance in such a fashion.

Then, astonishingly, a grudging respect overrode his simmering annoyance at being so easily
made the fool.

She was right on one point. He did need her
help.

"Very well, Miss Cresswell, you have my attention. How should I proceed?"

Two

Sarah had not desired to meet with Lord Chance. Despite her lack of social connections, even she had managed to hear of the Flawless Earl. Who had not? His every movement was a source of avid interest among the *ton*, his clothing discussed in the most exacting detail, and his discreet mistresses regarded with a sense of envy. She had expected him to be unbearably arrogant, and she had not been disappointed.

From the moment he had entered her home, he had regarded her with a cold disapproval he had taken no pains to hide. Not even his surprise that she was not quite the vulgar tart he had obviously been expecting had dulled the sneer in his voice or his patronizing air. Little wonder she had been unable to resist her devious trick.

And now it appeared he was suddenly willing to lower his aristocratic standards and allow her to offer her aid.

Sarah clenched her teeth. Drat it all. Why had she allowed Lord Scott to convince her to help this annoying gentleman?

Because you could never deny Lord Scott any request,

a small voice promptly reminded her. She owed him too much and cared too deeply.

And now . . . now she was obligated to help this gentleman who was gazing down his noble nose as if she were a nasty bit of goods he had discovered stuck to the bottom of his boots.

Well, she might be obligated to help him, but she did not intend to apologize for being the daughter of the Devilish Dandy. Nor did she intend to be bullied.

Folding her hands in her lap, she forced herself to meet his near-black gaze. An odd flutter raced through her stomach, the same flutter that had assaulted her when he first entered the room.

Sarah sternly squashed her foolish flight of fancy. She would concentrate only on the return of the Chance diamonds. The sooner she discovered them, the sooner this gentleman would be out of her life. "I shall need to know more of what occurred," she said in crisp tones.

He paused. Then, in a concise manner, he revealed his younger brother's troubles, leading to his rash theft of the jewels and the mysterious disappearance of them from the safe. Sarah listened in silence, her shrewd mind able to surmise a few facts Lord Chance conveniently neglected to mention. Facts such as the realization Ben had chosen a risky plot rather than turn to his brother for a loan, meaning Lord Chance was either clutch fisted or merely weary of pulling his brother out of trouble. She presumed the latter, since he had lowered himself to seek her help. Surely only a measure of guilt, even an unconscious measure of guilt, could have led him to her door. She also detected something else missing from his story, a fact that Lord Chance had obviously overlooked.

"Odd," she murmured as he came to a halt.

"What?"

Her chestnut brows drew together. "Was anything else stolen?"

"I do not believe so. Why?"

"If someone wished to steal your mother's jewels, why did they not do so when they were within her safe?" she demanded with unshakable logic. "After all, she no doubt has any number of other jewels of great value, and, of course, they could not have suspected your brother would take them on that precise evening."

There was a long pause as he considered her sensible words.

"Perhaps it was mere chance," he at last retorted. "They may have broken in simply because it was a convenient home and took what they could put their hands upon."

Sarah was swift to dismiss such a notion. Her years of living among the most talented and clever criminals made her regard the theft from the mind of the thief rather than the victim.

"If that were true, they would have grabbed the silver or your brother's purse. They certainly would not have taken the time to open the safe. The fact that they managed to elude the servants and open the safe without being captured implies planning and a certain skill." She pondered the problem for a long moment. "Such a risk without certainty of being rewarded. Would they have reason to believe your brother possessed anything of value?"

"No." He stroked a slender finger down the length of his jaw. "Indeed, my brother is renowned for never possessing a feather to fly with."

It was rather what she had suspected.

"Then only a fool would choose his home to enter," she pointed out, "unless they knew the diamonds would be there."

Clearly following her path of logic with commendable ease, Lord Chance gave a slow nod. "Yes."

"So who knew your brother possessed the diamonds?"

Lord Chance did not hesitate. "Maxwell."

Sarah could not prevent a small smile. Obviously the gentleman wished to believe the notorious Lord Maxwell was responsible, but she was not about to be readily swayed. She had heard the rumors surrounding Maxwell. Certainly he might bleed a young buck or blackmail an indiscreet lady, but he was not known through the back streets as a thief. Of course, a few well-placed questions would assure her one way or another. For now she wished to discover who else might have known of the diamonds.

"And your brother's staff," she murmured aloud.

"I hardly believe Ben would have confided his less than honorable intentions to his staff," he drawled in that soft tone which set her teeth on edge.

"Never underestimate servants," she could not resist informing him. "They know everything that occurs within their household."

As if sensing her irritation, he gave a mocking nod of his head. "I bow to your superior knowledge."

Sarah's ready humor banished her ill temper.

She supposed she had sounded unbearably top-lofty. Still, this gentleman could provoke the most patient of women.

"Did he confide in his friends?"

He gave a faint shrug. "I am forced to admit I do not know."

"We shall need to discover." Shifting toward the table in front of her, Sarah dropped the expensive stickpin and pulled forward the paper and quill she had prepared earlier. In a firm script, she began listing those with the knowledge to steal the diamonds. "We should also consider that one of the servants from your mother's establishment spied your brother taking the jewels. It would be a perfect opportunity to steal the diamonds without suspicion falling upon them."

He lifted his quizzing glass to regard her efforts. "That is quite a list."

"It is only a beginning."

"Where do you suggest I start first?"

Setting aside the quill, Sarah prepared herself for battle. It took little intelligence to realize Lord Chance was one of those gentlemen who preferred to be in command. He was bound to buck when she made her demands. "First we must come to an understanding."

"Indeed?" His voice was mild, but Sarah sensed a flare of amusement at her firm announcement.

"You know who I am," she said without apology. "You also know my childhood was decidedly untraditional."

"Yes."

"If I am to help you, then you must not question my methods nor attempt to interfere."

"You quite frighten me, Miss Cresswell." His

lips twitched as he stretched out his legs and crossed his glossy boots at the ankles. "Do you intend to be thoroughly dishonorable?"

Sarah was hard-pressed not to allow herself to smile. He might be aggravating, condescending, and arrogant to a fault, but she could not deny he possessed his share of charm.

"Not at all," she denied with what she hoped was her usual calm demeanor. "But I will be forced to travel through neighborhoods you would not approve of and at times pretend to be someone I am not."

His dark gaze made a thorough inspection of her well-defined features, lingering an odd moment on the generous curve of her mouth. "Why have you agreed to help me?" he abruptly demanded.

Unprepared for the question, Sarah gave a startled blink. "Lord Scott asked me," she said simply.

"And you always do what he asks of you?"

Sarah felt herself stiffen. She had no intention of discussing her relationship with Lord Scott with anyone. It was one of the few secrets she possessed, and one she intended to keep. "That is really none of your concern."

His gaze narrowed at her sharp tone, but, as if realizing she would not be pressed into confessing more, he gracefully retreated. Not that she believed for a moment that he had abandoned his curiosity. He was simply too wise for a frontal assault.

"Very well." He met her gaze squarely. "I have a few requests of my own."

Sarah was not at all surprised. It would be an ongoing battle for control.

"What are they?"

"I wish to be included in every aspect of the search."

Sarah gave a faint frown. For heaven's sake, she did not wish to be forever tripping over this gentleman. It would be bad enough to endure the occasional encounter. "You would only be in the way," she assured him in stern tones.

He dismissed her less than flattering remark with an elegant wave of his pale hand. "An unfortunate inconvenience, I fear. I will not waver from this point."

"You do not trust me?" she charged.

He pointedly glanced toward the diamond pin lying on the table. "You have effectively assured me I should trust no one."

This time Sarah could not prevent her impulsive laugh. "Touché."

His dark gaze appeared to be captured by the sudden lightening of her features. Then, with the faintest shake of his dark head, he slowly leaned forward. "Be assured, my dear, that while the Chance diamonds are quite valuable, my sole concern is protecting my mother from unnecessary heartbreak. I will do whatever necessary to assure her peace of mind."

She did not doubt his sincerity. He clearly cared a great deal about Lady Chance. "Very commendable."

"I must have those diamonds before Christmas."

"I shall do my best."

"As shall I." Lord Chance smoothly rose to his feet and crossed to Sarah. "I will return tomorrow."

Her eyes widened.

She had not agreed to allow him to be involved in her investigation. Certainly she did not wish to have him trailing behind her, interfering in her business. But the distinct challenge in his midnight gaze made her hold her tongue. He seemed to dare her to decline his presence, as if she were uncertain of her skill.

Sarah predictably bristled with annoyance. She might not always appreciate her odd upbringing, but she did know she possessed all the skills necessary to retrieve the diamonds. She would show this gentleman she was more than a match for a common thief. "Very well, my lord."

His first genuine smile softened his features as he slowly reached down to grasp her hand and lift it to his lips. "You are quite an extraordinary woman, Miss Cresswell," he murmured. Then, as Sarah sat there stunned by his unpredictable behavior, he turned to leave the room.

Absently rubbing her hand, which tingled from the heat of his lips, she decided Lord Scott had a great deal to answer for.

Surely he had realized Lord Chance was precisely the sort of gentleman to stir her usually placid temperament.

But then, perhaps that had been his intention, she acknowledged with a flare of insight. On how many occasions had he chastised her for being far too content with her independence for a lady of five and twenty? He charged her brisk competency frightened away prospective suitors.

Sarah had always dismissed his lectures. It did not matter if her independence or her connection to the Devilish Dandy had kept any prospective suitors far from her door. She had learned to accept her role as a spinster and was deter-

mined to be content with her lot. After all, she
had her home, her work at a local school for the
underprivileged, and, of course, her younger sisters, Emma and Rachel.

Her life was quite filled, she assured herself, and
the last thing she desired or needed was a gentleman such as Lord Chance creating difficulties.

With a suddenly brisk motion, Sarah rose to
her feet. Good heavens, what was she thinking?
Lord Chance would hardly be in her life long
enough to create difficulties. Once she had located the Chance diamonds, she would never
view his handsome face again. A thought, she assured herself, that filled her with absolute joy.

Ignoring the diamond stickpin still lying on the
table, Sarah moved from the room. She certainly
possessed more productive things to do with her
time than brood upon Lord Chance. Turning toward the stairs that led to her chambers, she was
abruptly halted by the distinct sound of whistling
coming from her small library.

More startled than frightened, Sarah promptly
veered to cross the hall and step into the narrow
room lined with bookcases and boasting a fine
Louis XIV writing desk.

"Watts?" she called, expecting the always alert
butler to be hovering near in the event she might
need his ready fist. It was not Watts, however, who
suddenly stepped from behind the velvet curtain.

Sarah stood frozen in shock. The gentleman
had changed since she had last clapped eyes
upon him. His tall frame was leaner, his brown
hair streaked with gray had grown longer and was
gathered at the neck with a black ribbon, a full
mustache covered his upper lip, and a black satin
eye patch was placed over one eye. But for all

the changes there was no mistaking the Devilish Dandy. "Father."

"Good morning, my dearest." He offered her an elegant bow.

"What are you doing here?"

Although not precisely a handsome man, Solomon Cresswell possessed a rakish air and an elegance of style that had allowed him to charm his way into the highest circles of Society. Attired in a striped coat with a fall of lace at his wrists and in shoes with jeweled buckles, he appeared a veritable dandy rather than a desperate criminal in hiding.

"You did not believe I would abandon my beloved daughters," the intruder demanded with a distinct glint of amusement in his green eyes. Or at least in the eye he had not covered with the absurd patch.

Her shock slowly faded, to be replaced with anger. Really, for a grown gentleman he could be remarkably foolish. "Have you taken leave of your senses?" She moved to stand in the center of the room. "If you are captured . . ."

"Fah." With supreme indifference, Solomon measured a pinch of snuff from his emerald-encrusted box. "Those imbecile runners will never outwit the Devilish Dandy."

"They have little need of wits if you deliberately walk into their arms," Sarah said in dry tones. "I thought you had fled to India."

"India? Egads." He gave a dramatic shudder. "I should as soon remain at Newgate. No, I merely left a few clumsy clues so those chasing me would blunder about while I slipped quietly into the country."

A sharp pang twisted Sarah's heart at the mention of Newgate. She still awoke in the middle of the night from dreams of her father in that horrible place. "Why did you not remain there?"

"Really, Sarah, I presumed that you would be delighted to have the company of your father."

"Not when most of London would dearly love to place a noose about your neck," she retorted.

The Devilish Dandy merely laughed. "As charmingly blunt as ever, eh, Sarah?"

"Merely practical."

Strolling forward, Solomon regarded her with a critical eye. "I see you are wearing my necklace," he said, referring to the sapphire pendant about her neck. It had arrived shortly after his disappearance, along with an emerald pendant for Emma and a ruby pendant for Rachel. "It is just as beautiful on you as I had hoped, although I cannot say the same for that gown. Truly, my dearest, you could be a splendidly handsome woman if you would just halt this foolish notion of behaving as a spinster."

Sarah took no offense at her father's chastisement. He had been forever attempting to encourage his daughters to follow in his flamboyant footsteps. Sarah and Emma had firmly resisted, preferring a quietly modest existence. Rachel, however, had inherited her father's reckless spirit as well as his charm, a fact that had given Sarah more than one sleepless night.

Sarah gave a faint shrug. "I am a spinster."

"Nonsense. You simply have not encountered a gentleman whom is capable of stealing your heart." A speculative gleam entered his blue eyes. "Of course, if any gentleman were worthy of my daughter, it would be the Flawless Earl."

Sarah was forced to battle the most ridiculous

urge to blush. Goodness, what was it about Lord Chance that disturbed her usual calm?

"Lord Chance was merely here to seek my advice," she retorted in repressive tones.

Solomon was undaunted. "Why would a wealthy lord seek your advice?"

"We are not discussing Lord Chance."

"No?"

"No." She placed her hands on her hips. "We are discussing your return to the country before you are discovered."

"Bah. I have no stomach for such bucolic surroundings." He regarded her with an oddly knowing gaze, as if he sensed she was hiding something from him. "Besides which, I have a certain premonition you are in need of my presence."

"Why will you not accept that it is far too dangerous?" she demanded in exasperation.

"What is life without danger?"

"Peaceful."

"Absurd." He dismissed her suggestion with a shrug. "Besides, I am in disguise."

She regarded him with raised brows. "What disguise?"

He tapped the ridiculous eye patch. "You do not see before you the Devilish Dandy. Instead I am your Uncle Pierre recently arrived from France." He swept an elegant bow. *"Enchante, ma enfant."*

She gazed at him in disbelief. Although less than a handful could actually identify Solomon Cresswell with any certainty, those few would not be misled by a change of hair, a mustache, and an eye patch. It was ludicrous.

"You must be jesting?"

"Not at all."

"No one will believe you are some mythical French uncle."

He lifted his hand to his heart in a wounded fashion. "You underestimate my acting skills, Sarah. I can make people believe whatever I wish them to believe. It truly is a pity I did not turn my talents to the stage. I should no doubt have made Kean cry with envy."

Sarah gave a shake of her head. "I do not doubt your acting skills, Father, but this is no stage."

"Do not fear, my dearest. I shall be perfectly safe." His expression became uncharacteristically stern. "Now tell me of Lord Chance."

Her father rarely used such a tone with her, preferring to allow his daughters to more or less have their way. Sarah heaved a sigh. There would be no distracting him now. "Someone stole his mother's diamonds and he wishes to retrieve them," she said in clipped tones.

The Devilish Dandy gave a low whistle. "The Chance diamonds. Well, well."

"Do not even think of it, Father."

"Why, Sarah, I am wounded," he retorted with a sniff. "You are gazing upon a reformed gentleman."

"Poppycock."

Again the room was filled with the Devilish Dandy's laughter. "Well, perhaps not thoroughly reformed, but I will admit my brush with the noose has made me realize I was growing decidedly too old for such capers. Now I only wish to be a comfort to my daughters in my advancing years."

Sarah was far from convinced. Her father was a born rogue. "Very pretty."

"Ah, I see I shall have to prove myself." He accepted her suspicions with ease. "My first task shall be to lend my aid in your effort to help Lord Chance."

Her eyes widened in dismay. The Devilish Dandy and Lord Chance together? The mere thought was enough to make her break out in a rash.

"Absolutely not."

He blinked at her fierce tone. "Who better to locate a jewel thief than a jewel thief?"

"I am perfectly capable of locating the jewels on my own . . ."

She bit off her low words as Watts abruptly stepped into the room. The butler revealed only the vaguest hint of surprise at the sight of his former master.

"Pardon me, miss, but Mrs. Surton is here to see you. She refuses to leave."

"Oh . . . damn." Sarah threw her hands up in frustration. Mrs. Surton was the leading patron of the school Sarah had founded and an endless source of irritation. Not a day passed that she was not arriving upon her doorstep with some officious demand or some complaint of Sarah's inadequacies. As a rule, Sarah accepted her unpleasant companionship with a calm grace. After all, the woman did donate a great deal of money to the school and just as importantly bullied every other matron of Society to follow her example. Sarah considered the woman's rudeness a small price to pay for keeping the school doors open. At the moment, however, she was in little mood for the woman. "I shall have to see her." She pointed a finger directly into her father's thin countenance. "You stay here."

"But, my dear . . ."

"Stay."

With one last warning glare, Sarah turned on her heel and marched from the room.

So far today she had endured an arrogant lord, a renegade father, and now an overbearing tartar. *Perhaps I should be the one to retire to the country,* she acknowledged ruefully. Feeding chickens and tending a garden had never seemed so appealing.

Three

Mrs. Surton was a tall, gaunt woman with sour features and an unfortunate manner of speaking her mind. It was generally conceded that her timid husband had hastened to his grave to avoid her poisonous tongue, a rumor Sarah readily believed.

Still, for all the woman's annoying faults, Sarah could not deny her school had flourished because of Mrs. Surton's generosity. From a cramped cellar with five students, they had moved to a refurbished warehouse with thirty students and three teachers as well as a kitchen that served a much needed meal to the poor children. Sarah had assured herself she could endure the cutting remarks and endless rudeness to save so many children from the streets. That, however, did not make it any more pleasant to receive daily visits from the obnoxious woman.

On entering the foyer, she found Mrs. Surton bristling with impatience. As usual, she was attired in forbidding black, her thin brown hair scraped into a knot. Her narrow features could have been chiseled from stone as she watched Sarah approach.

"Mrs. Surton," Sarah murmured.

The woman's thin lips nearly disappeared. "Do you realize that ruffian you have hired as a butler attempted to have me turned away?"

Sarah swallowed a smile. Watts had been a top bruiser in his day, knocking out no less than fifty-seven men. He had saved her father on countless occasions and had proved to be a valuable source of protection for a maiden on her own. But not even he could prove a match for Mrs. Surton. "I fear I have been suffering from a headache and requested that Watts announce that I was unavailable."

Far from sympathetic, Mrs. Surton regarded her in an accusing fashion. "I never suffer from headaches. I hope you are not of a sickly constitution."

"Not at all."

"Good. It would not be at all convenient if you were always taking to bed with some malady."

Sarah was in full agreement. She had never pretended to be fashionably delicate, but instead maintained a robust constitution that was hardly seemly for a maiden.

"Is there something you need?" She attempted to bring the conversation to the point of Mrs. Surton's visit. On a normal day, she found Mrs. Surton's presence annoying. On a day with her father just upstairs, she found her presence nerve shattering. She did not trust the Devilish Dandy any farther than she could toss him.

Mrs. Surton sniffed at her abrupt tone, but thankfully allowed herself to be diverted. "I wished to inform you that Lady Milhouse has agreed to become a sponsor for the school."

Sarah did not need to pretend her flare of

pleasure. Lady Milhouse was not only extremely wealthy, she was also of a social position to ensure that where she led, others would soon follow. Her patronage would certainly inspire further donations.

"That is wonderful."

"Yes. It shall mean we will be able to take in at least five more students."

"I shall have them there by the end of the week," Sarah promised.

"We might also be in the position to purchase a few coats and boots for the children if we practice the utmost economy."

"Of course."

"I hope tomorrow that you . . . Oh."

The officious words stumbled to a halt as Mrs. Surton glanced over Sarah's shoulder. A deep foreboding filled Sarah's stomach as she slowly turned to view her father mincing down the stairs with a smile she knew all too well. The Devilish Dandy was intent on mischief, and there wasn't a bloody thing she could do to halt him.

"*Ma petite,*" he drawled in an outrageous French accent, "why do you hover in this so damp foyer? Surely your guest would be more comfortable in the salon?"

Rigid with fury, she flashed her father a speaking glare. "Mrs. Surton was just leaving."

"Before we have been introduced?" Solomon protested with a wicked grin. "*Mon Dieu,* it shall not be." Turning, he offered the startled visitor a lavish bow. "Allow me, madam. I am Monsieur Valmere, Miss Cresswell's uncle, recently come to London from Paris."

Sarah held her breath, awaiting Mrs. Surton to pronounce him as the Devilish Dandy, or at the

very least protest at being forced into an introduction with a member of Sarah's less than respectable family. But, shockingly, the tatar
appeared as flustered as a schoolgirl by the attentions of the flamboyant Frenchman. There was
even the faintest hint of a blush on the angular
cheekbones.

"Oh . . . I did not realize that Miss Cresswell
possessed French relations," she simpered.

"Only through marriage. I was wed to her father's sister."

Seeming to have forgotten Sarah, the older
woman batted her stubby lashes. "I see."

"Unfortunately, my dearest wife passed some
years ago. To relieve my loneliness, I sought the
companionship of Sarah. She has kindly agreed
to introduce me to her friends—although I did
not realize her friends would be quite so lovely."

Sarah blinked in amazement as Mrs. Surton uttered a shrill giggle. Before this moment, she
would have bet every quid she possessed that Mrs.
Surton did not even know how to giggle.

"Uncle Pierre," she gritted out through a stiff
smile, "Mrs. Surton and I are rather occupied at
the moment."

"Nonsense," Mrs. Surton interrupted, her gaze
never leaving the Devilish Dandy's countenance.

Sarah smothered a sigh. She had witnessed that
bemused expression on too many occasions not
to recognize the symptoms of yet another female
felled by the dashing charm of Solomon Cresswell. Egads, Mrs. Surton did not even seem to
mind the waxed mustache and absurd eye patch.

"We can easily postpone our discussion until
later."

"*Bien,* allow me to escort you to the salon. Far

more comfortable than this drafty hall." With exquisite care, he placed Mrs. Surton's hand upon his arm and began leading her up the stairs. At the same moment, Watts appeared on the landing. "Ah, Watts, you will kindly bring your best ratafia."

"At once, monsieur."

Stone-faced, Watts headed down the stairs, pausing at Sarah's side as she glared at her father's retreating back.

"There shall be no need for a noose, Watts," she muttered. "I shall strangle him myself."

After leaving Miss Cresswell's, Lord Chance had enjoyed a busy day. He had called on his tailor, stepped into his club, attended a private lecture on Egyptian artifacts, and devoted a few hours to a charming musicale. But while the activities had been pleasurable enough, he could not deny his thoughts had been persistently occupied with meeting the Devilish Dandy's daughter.

Perhaps not surprising, he had forced himself to concede. She was without a doubt the most unusual woman he had ever encountered. Not once had she giggled or blushed beneath his piercing regard, and certainly there had been nothing remotely flirtatious in her manner. Indeed, she had met him stare for stare and thrust for thrust. Not once had he felt he held the upper hand in the encounter. A most unusual situation.

With an odd sense of anticipation, Chance arose from his bed the next morning and attired himself in a warm coat of dark burgundy and a silver waistcoat. He even took special pains with his cravat before daring the chilled November air. It was still quite early when he made his way up the stairs of Miss Cresswell's home, but the door was readily pulled open and he was allowed to enter the foyer uncontested. "Good morning, Watts," he murmured as he handed over his coat and hat.

"Good morning, my lord. Miss Cresswell is in the salon."

"I shall see myself in."

Climbing the stairs, he pushed open the door to the salon and entered the room. He had expected to discover Miss Cresswell once again seated on the sofa awaiting his arrival. He discovered instead a young lad attired in one of his own groom's uniforms.

Just for a moment, Chance gazed at the stranger with a suspicious frown. Then, with a sharp stab of disbelief, he realized beneath the heavy uniform and powered wig was not a young servant, but Miss Cresswell. "Good gads," he muttered, a frown forming on his wide brow.

There was a distinct sparkle in her blue eyes. "Welcome, my lord."

"Where the blazes did you get my groom's uniform?"

"No questions, my lord," she reminded him.

Chance discovered himself strangely discomposed. He had expected Miss Cresswell to be less than conventional, but he certainly hadn't expected this. At the moment, he could not decide whether to be furious at her audacity or admire her cunning. In the end, he could not prevent a rather wry smile. "May I at least inquire why you are attired as my groom?"

"Certainly," she graciously conceded. "I desire you to drive to your brother's home so you might gather a list of those who knew he possessed the diamonds."

Chance was quite certain there was something far more devious to her plan than a simple visit to his brother's.

"Surely that does not require you to be my groom?"

"Of course it does." Moving forward, she managed to capture the loose-limbed gait of a young lad. Chance felt a prick of admiration at her skill. Had he not known with absolute certainty there was a very fine female form beneath that uniform, he might have been fooled himself. "While you are distracting your brother and the various servants who must attend to a guest, I shall make my appearance in the kitchen and distract the remaining staff. At that point, Lucky will search the servant's quarters for the missing diamonds."

Chance was almost afraid to inquire. "Lucky?"

Without warning, a thin urchin with a shock of black hair and dark eyes stepped away from the wall. Chance silently cursed his inattention. He had never even noticed the lad. With a narrowed gaze, he watched as the child of thirteen or fourteen strolled to Miss Cresswell's side.

"My father won him in a card game," Miss Cresswell explained. Then, as Chance's features predictably tightened, she gave a low chuckle. "Oh, you needn't look so pious. His previous employer was a reprehensible brute, and Lucky was quite happy to become a member of our household. My father claimed he brought us a good deal of fortune, and so his name."

Chance gave a slow shake of his head, wondering if Miss Cresswell weren't a bit mad. "Surely you do not propose to have a mere boy search my brother's home?" he demanded.

Miss Cresswell reached out to place a slender hand on the urchin's shoulder. "Of course. Lucky is extraordinarily talented in slipping about unnoted, besides which he possesses a sharp wit that is never rattled. I haven't the least doubt he shall someday make his fortune upon the 'Change."

Chance did not doubt the boy's ability. He possessed an odd maturity for one so young and there was a decided glint of intelligence in the dark eyes. Still, that did not ease his concern in involving a mere child in such a dangerous scheme. "That is all very well, but what if he is caught?"

Lucky abruptly stepped forward. "Begging your pardon, sir, but no one can catch me unless I wish to be caught," he said with unshakable confidence.

"He is quite right," Miss Cresswell concurred, her lips twitching with a hint of humor. "How else could I possess this uniform?"

Chance felt himself stiffen. Miss Cresswell possessed the audacity to have this child break into his own home? The woman was beyond impertinent. She was . . . Words failed him as his own sense of humor thrust aside his initial irritation. He was not such a poor sport that he could not appreciate being bested, even by a chit who was far too clever for her own good.

"I hope he did not help himself to any other of my belongings," he drawled.

"No, sir," Lucky protested in indignant tones.

"That was quite unworthy, my lord." Miss Cresswell offered him a chastising glance. "Lucky is a fine boy and was only following my directions."

Chance was far from contrite. He was beginning to wonder just what he had gotten himself into. "Did it occur to you that you had only to ask me to acquire the uniform?"

That twinkle returned to her blue eyes. "Yes, it occurred to me. It also occurred to me your natural instinct would have you conveniently forgetting to bring it with you today."

He wasn't about to admit she was absolutely right. It was quite disturbing enough to have been surprised by her transformation. Had he been given the opportunity to consider her scheme, he would certainly have put a firm end to it. Now he could merely shrug. "What a poor opinion you have of me, my dear."

"Then you have no objections to my plan?"

A wry smile touched his lips. "Several, but I am quickly becoming of the opinion that I should only be wasting my breath."

"Quite true," she retorted in firm tones.

"And a promise is a promise," he reluctantly forced himself to concede.

"Very well. Shall we go?"

Although located in an elegant neighborhood, Ben's town house was rather cramped and sparsely furnished. Ben had little interest and fewer funds to create a showplace. Still, for a gentleman on his own, it was an adequate establishment that was well situated.

Seated in the library, Lord Chance watched through narrowed lids as his younger brother paced the patterned carpet. He discovered it surprisingly difficult to concentrate on his simple task with the knowledge that Miss Cresswell and Lucky were currently established below stairs. Perhaps not so surprising, he conceded with an inward grimace. A gentleman in his position could hardly be accustomed to young women who readily posed as grooms nor urchins who slipped in and out of homes uninvited. But while he might not approve of such tactics, he could not deny it was a clever scheme.

Recalling his own small contribution to the plan, he tapped impatient fingers on the arm of his chair. "Think, Ben," he charged in low tones.

"I am," Ben muttered, turning about to retrace his steps. "It was all such a muddle. Goldie and I went to Mother's to get the jewels . . ."

"And no servants witnessed you?" Chance interrupted as he thought of Miss Cresswell's words.

"No, Goldie was keeping watch. Then we came straight here and put the jewels in the safe . . . Oh, I say."

"What is it?" Chance demanded.

With his brow furrowed Ben struggled to recall the events of the fateful evening.

"We were putting the jewels in the safe when Moreland and Fritz called."

Chance was only vaguely acquainted with the two dandies. From what little he did know the two were much in the same mold as Ben's friend Lord Goldmar, more affectionately known as Goldie. They all possessed a fashionable lack of intelligence and love for madcap dares. They were also notorious for living well beyond their means.

"Did they see the jewels?"

Ben gave an emphatic shake of his head. "No,

I went to distract them while Goldie locked the safe. It was still locked when I went to bed that evening."

Chance was not nearly so confident. He intended to keep a close guard on Ben's supposed friends.

"And you told no one you possessed the jewels?" Chance pressed.

A rather uncomfortable expression fluttered across Ben's youthful countenance.

"I might have mentioned them to Fiona."

"Your mistress?" Chance allowed his expression to thin.

"She did not take them, if that is what you are thinking," Ben retorted in defensive tones. "I won't have a word said against her."

Chance had many words that he might have said, but he contented himself with adding Fiona's name to the growing list of suspects. "What of Goldie? Could he have told anyone?"

Ben stiffened at the accusation. "Good Lord, no. Right as they come."

"Someone took the jewels," Chance pointed out in dry tones.

"Certainly. Some scandalous thief who broke in while I slept."

"A thief who was well aware those jewels were in your possession."

It took a long moment for comprehension to dawn in Ben's eyes. "Oh."

Chance gave a humorless smile. "Yes."

Clearly disturbed by the realization, Ben gave a sharp shake of his head.

"Fah. Must be bloody daft to think one of my friends was involved."

"But one was," Chance stated in tones that defied argument.

"You only say that because you have always disliked my companions," Ben charged.

"I do not dislike your companions," Chance denied, his expression grim. "But I do think they are fribbles with few morals, and I do not doubt for a moment they would stoop to any level if they were desperate enough."

A mulish expression descended upon Ben's face, but before he could voice his arguments, the portly butler entered the room.

"Pardon me, sir, but Lord Chance's groom requested I remind him he has an appointment at half past the hour."

Chance smoothly rose to his feet. He had to presume Lucky had completed his search and somehow alerted Miss Cresswell.

"Thank you," he said toward the butler. Then, as the servant discreetly retreated, he turned back toward his flushed brother. "I wish you to write down a list of everyone who might even have suspected you possessed the Chance diamonds and have it sent to me." He regarded his brother in his most forbidding manner. "And, Ben, do not allow foolish loyalty to blind you. I want every name."

The flush deepened, but Ben was all too aware he was in a precarious position. For the moment, he could only do as Chance commanded him. "Very well."

With a last warning glance, Chance left the room and made his way down to the front door. Retrieving his coat and hat from the butler, he stepped into the chill November wind. For a moment he paused as the breeze threatened to tum-

ble his beaver hat from his head. Then, before
he could continue his path down the stairs, he
was halted by the sight of a maid hurrying from
around the house toward his waiting carriage.
With a faint sense of surprise, he watched her
furtive movements, wondering what she could be
about as she halted beside Miss Cresswell, who
was holding open the carriage door as a proper
groom. It was not until he noted the budding
infatuation on the maid's pretty face that he realized the truth.

The maid had clearly been smitten by his supposed groom.

"A moment, Samuel," the maid pleaded, her
voice inviting. "I have brought you a cake."

A dark flush stained Miss Cresswell's features
as she awkwardly shook of her head. "Oh, no. I
could not."

"But I insist," the maid pleaded.

"Really, I would rather not."

"Please take it . . . for me."

Clearly trapped, Miss Cresswell reluctantly accepted the small cake. "Thank you."

"Perhaps we shall meet again," the maid per-
sisted. "I have half days on the last Wednesday
of the month."

"Oh, I don't think . . ."

"We could go for a walk, or perhaps have tea."

"I . . . well . . ."

Finding an inordinate amount of humor in the
situation, Chance swept down the stairs and
climbed into the carriage.

Settling himself on the velvet squabs, Chance
peered down his long nose with a smug superi-
ority. "If you have finished seducing the local
maids, Samuel, I would appreciate being on our

way. I do not care to sit in this frigid air all morning."

Her blue eyes flashed as the carriage door was snapped shut. Then, as Miss Cresswell climbed next to his rightful groom, Chance tilted back his head to laugh with a great deal of enjoyment.

Four

Sarah gritted her teeth as the carriage briskly set off from the town house. She felt a fool.

Who the blazes would have suspected that her brief charade would cause such an awkward situation? For goodness sakes, the maid must be daft to even glance in her direction. And then to have Lord Chance fully aware of her predicament . . . Really, it could not be more provoking.

Then, as swiftly as her annoyance had arisen, it was tempered by her ready sense of the ridiculous.

In all fairness, it was a humorous situation. Indeed, had the events been reversed, she would certainly have found his discomfort vastly amusing. Not that anyone could ever possibly mistake his shockingly masculine form as that of a woman, even if he were clothed in hoops, she wryly acknowledged.

Still, she wished the maid had not followed her to the carriage. It had been embarrassing enough to endure her blatant flirtations in the kitchen without having Lord Chance as an audience.

Her exasperated thoughts were thankfully interrupted as a small lad stepped into the street.

"Please halt," she commanded the genuine groom, hastily scrambling down from her perch. With swift movements, she pulled open the carriage door and both she and Lucky tucked themselves inside. Just as swiftly, the carriage was once again on its way. Settled upon the seat, she was reluctantly forced to glance across the carriage to where Lord Chance sat very much at his leisure. Not surprisingly, his dark eyes still harbored a devilish glint. With her usual straightforward manner, Sarah folded her hands in her lap and met his gaze squarely. "I am happy that I could provide you with so much amusement, my lord."

"You did indeed," he readily admitted. "I do not believe I have ever seen a maiden so swiftly smitten."

"Cor, yes." Lucky was anxious to join in the jest, a wide smile splitting his thin face. "You should have seen the goose batting her lashes and plying the Miss with scones and such. It were a proper sight to behold."

Sarah struggled to banish the blush that threatened to rise. "Yes, it was all very amusing."

Pressing his hands to his chest Lucky fluttered his lashes in an outrageous fashion. "Oh, Samuel, you must have some tea," he squeaked in a high tone. "And I made these scones myself."

Lord Chance tilted back his head to laugh with rich enjoyment. "I am quite in awe of your fatal attractions, my dear. You harbor a potent weapon to the members of the fairer sex."

Sarah's own expression was sour. "It was all a great deal of nonsense. The maid is clearly of a romantic disposition and anxious to attract the interest of any gentleman within sight."

His dark gaze lingered on her unconsciously

pink cheeks. "Do you not believe in love at first sight . . . Samuel?"

"Miss Cresswell says only lobbies believe in love," Lucky obligingly chimed in.

The earl's dark gaze never swayed. "How very cynical. I thought all maidens were desperate to tumble into love."

Sarah unwittingly squared her shoulders. "You are mistaken, my lord. I am quite satisfied with my life as it is."

"Perhaps that is because you have yet to meet a gentleman worthy of your heart," Lord Chance softly drawled.

Sarah's breath caught as Lucky gave a sage nod of his head. "That's the right of it, sir," he quipped. "Only the very best gent would be proper for Miss Cresswell. She's a rare 'un."

Lord Chance gave a slow nod of his head. "A rare one, indeed."

Nearly lost in the compelling beauty of his eyes, Sarah gave a sharp shake of her head. What was the matter with her? Lord Chance was merely roasting her. He would begin to think she was as fanciful as that maid if she did not collect her wits.

"Enough of this foolishness," she forced herself to mutter. "Did you find anything, Lucky?"

Thankfully diverted, the boy gave an expressive grimace. "Nothing of interest. The butler has a stash of the best brandy, the housekeeper is hiding the silver beneath her bed, and a footman has a horde of chocolate."

"Good gads," Lord Chance uttered in obvious surprise.

Far more accustomed to life below stairs, Sarah merely shrugged. "But no jewels?"

"No, and nothing out of the ordinary to prove anyone has come into a fortune."

Sarah nibbled her lower lip as she considered the information. She did not doubt Lucky had been extremely thorough in his search. If the jewels or any overt symbols of wealth had been in the house, Lucky would have discovered them.

"We must consider what is to be done next," she announced, refusing to acknowledge the tiny flutter in her stomach was anything but annoyance at the knowledge Lord Chance was destined to be in her life for at least the next few days.

With his casual elegance Lord Chance leaned back into his seat. "I propose we look to Maxwell. He is the most likely suspect."

Sarah gave a rather wry smile. "I fear I have not precisely devised the means of investigating Lord Maxwell."

"Lucky should be able to swiftly discover if he has the jewels or not," Lord Chance pointed out, clearly forgetting his earlier distaste at allowing a young boy to take such a risk.

In truth, the notion had crossed Sarah's mind as well, but she had reluctantly dismissed such an easy solution.

"Lord Maxwell is far too clever to keep the jewels in his town house, especially if he realizes that suspicion is bound to fall upon him," she said. "If he did take them, he would be sure to place them somewhere that could not be connected with himself."

"Unless he has already sold them," Lord Chance retorted in grim tones.

"I have already started inquiries among those who would be approached in such matters. If someone in London has thus far attempted to sell such famous diamonds, we shall soon know."

His lean features regained their sardonic amusement at her crisp tone. "Once again you are a step ahead of me, Miss Cresswell." His head tilted to one side. "What do you propose we do now?"

Sarah hesitated a moment before she allowed herself to concede the next logical course of action. "I believe we should call upon your mother," she reluctantly admitted.

Expecting him to adamantly refuse to allow her anywhere near his mother's establishment, Sarah was caught off guard when he gave a decisive nod of his head.

"Very well." His dark gaze took a thorough survey of her ridiculous uniform. "But you will not go there as my groom."

Sarah frowned in surprise. "Why ever not?"

A mocking smile curved his lips. "For one thing, I do not believe the maids could bear the heartache of encountering the irresistible Samuel."

Her lips thinned. "Do you have a better notion?"

"Yes," he retorted in that soft, utterly superior voice. "You shall accompany me."

"Absurd," Sarah burst out before she could halt the words. "You cannot introduce me to your mother."

His masculine features remained unruffled. "We shall say I discovered you beside the road after you had badly twisted your ankle and naturally, being a noble gentleman, I rushed to your aid. From there I carried you to the nearest home, which just happened to be my mother's."

For some reason the image of this gentleman carrying her anywhere made her heart miss a strategic beat. With an effort, she sternly reminded herself that sensible young ladies did not wish to be carried off—especially not by arrogant, high-handed gentlemen, even if they were insufferably handsome.

"I was walking without a maid?" she demanded, hoping she at least appeared sensible.

Lord Chance shrugged. "Of course, you sent her to fetch your carriage."

"And what of Lucky?"

"He will possess ample opportunity to search while the servants fuss over your injury."

Sarah gazed at the stubborn lord, wishing she could discover some fault to his plan. She did not like having another in command. "You do your mother no service in forcing an introduction to the daughter of the Devilish Dandy." She at last fell upon her last defense.

Predictably, he merely favored her with that lazy smile. "I have little doubt that my mother will take an instant liking to you. She possesses a decided weakness for outspoken, saucy young wenches."

Sarah stiffened. What the devil did he mean? She was calm, logical, and utterly practical. "I am not saucy."

"Only when provoked," he conceded softly.

"Which seems to happen only in your presence, sir," she said tartly.

The earl's dark eyes deliberately narrowed. "Now that, Miss Cresswell, is a most intriguing remark."

Their gazes tangled, and just for a moment both forgot the young lad watching them with shrewd comprehension. Then Lucky gave a sudden laugh. "Cor, I thought she would plant you a facer for sure, guv. Not many stands up to the Miss."

Wholly unrepentant, Lord Chance slowly smiled. "Perhaps it is time that someone did."

"You, sir?" Lucky slyly demanded.

"We shall see," he murmured. Then, as the carriage rumbled to a halt, he abruptly turned to glance out the window. "Here we are. I shall call again tomorrow."

Saucy.

He had possessed the audacity to label her as saucy.

Entering her tiny home, Sarah resisted the urge to glance back at the glossy carriage and stick out her tongue.

Really, the gentleman was . . . Sarah was at a loss to properly describe the aggravating Lord Chance.

It was not as if she couldn't take a bit of jesting, she assured herself.

With her distinctly odd upbringing, she had long ago discovered if she did not laugh at the absurdities in life she would grow to be a bitter woman indeed, something she was determined to avoid at all cost.

But Lord Chance seemed to possess an uncanny ability to prick through her hard-earned composure to the more vulnerable woman beneath. That fact disturbed her more than she cared to acknowledge.

Decidedly ruffled, Sarah marched up the stairs, anxious to remove the uniform, which had begun to itch. She had just reached the first landing when a faint noise drew her into the front salon. A sudden frown marred her features at the sight of two young maidens seated upon the sofa.

Drat, she silently seethed.

Her busy morning had effectively dismissed the memory that she had sent a message to both of her sisters to ask them to join her this afternoon. Now they had arrived, and she did not feel at all prepared to face them.

For a moment, Sarah silently studied her younger sisters. As always, Emma was sensibly attired in a gray gown, her honey-colored curls scraped into a bun at the nape of her neck, her pure green eyes dark with concern. Only the emerald pendant about her neck gave a hint of color.

Poor Emma had perhaps suffered the greatest beneath the taint attached to the Cresswell name, Sarah acknowledged. Her brief attempt at a Season had ended in shame when Solomon had been publicly arrested as the Devilish Dandy. Of course, even before then Emma had always felt a measure of shame for being related to the less than honorable family. Sarah had tried her best to ease the young girl's troubled guilt, but she always feared she had failed the most sensitive child.

Rachel, in contrast, was every inch the daughter of the Devilish Dandy. A tiny beauty with golden curls and mischievous hazel eyes, she boldly faced Society with enough wit and charm that only the highest sticklers turned her aside. She had also, unfortunately, inherited her father's lust for adventure and kept Sarah in constant dread that one of her madcap dares would

land her in scandal that not even her charm
could save her from.

At last sensing her presence, both maidens
turned to regard Sarah. Not surprisingly, Rachel
laughed at her odd attire, while Emma widened
her eyes in shock.

"Sarah . . . good heavens," Emma murmured.
"Why ever are you dressed as a servant?"

Not prepared to discuss her search for the
Chance diamonds and certainly not her current
connection to Lord Chance, Sarah merely
shrugged. "Please do not ask."

Rachel tilted her head to one side, her eyes
dancing with amusement. "I think it quite becomes you. If you were not my sister, I should
set my cap for you."

The jest was too vivid a reminder of Lord
Chance's teasing for Sarah to readily join in her
sister's amusement. "As witty as ever, Rachel," she
said dryly, her gaze taking in the poppy-colored
Indian muslin gown with a neckline that revealed
a great deal too much ivory skin as well as a perfect ruby pendant. "And as scandalously clad."

Impervious to her sister's chiding, Rachel
tossed her golden curls. "At least I am not clad
as a groom."

Clicking her tongue impatiently, Emma leaned
forward. "Why did you ask us to come here,
Sarah?"

Why, indeed. Sarah drew in a deep breath. Her
announcement was bound to create a furor.
Hardly surprising. Everything that had to do with
the Devilish Dandy created a furor. "I thought
you should know Father has returned to London."

A shocked, brittle silence descended before Emma surged to her feet.

"Returned?" she uttered in dismay. "He is here?"

Rachel also rose to her feet, but rather than dismay, her lovely face was illuminated by a brilliant smile. "I knew he would not go to that horrid India," she exclaimed. "Where is he? Can I see him?"

That was a question Sarah preferred not to ponder. "I have not seen him since breakfast."

Emma unconsciously twisted her hands together. "What is he doing here?"

"Currently he is pretending to be Uncle Pierre from Paris," Sarah said, her smile wry.

"This is horrid."

"Horrid?" Rachel favored her sister with a dark glance. "What a milksop you are, Emma. I think it is perfectly marvelous to have Father home again."

Emma stiffened in resentment. "Oh yes, there is nothing more enjoyable than being the source of ridicule and gossip throughout London."

"Fiddlesticks."

Anxious to ward off a sisterly squabble, Sarah lifted a slender hand. "Please, let us not argue. I simply wished you both to be aware of Father's return to London."

"I thank you, Sarah," Emma said in low tones, drawing on her gloves with less than steady hands. "Now I must take my leave. I have no desire to encounter Father."

She moved toward the door, but as she passed, Sarah reached out to lay a detaining hand on her arm. "Emma . . . you must try not to be so unforgiving. He is your father," Sarah said softly.

Emma's green eyes abruptly blazed with a pain that time had not yet healed. "It is not so simple."

"No," Sarah agreed softly.

"I must go."

"A moment." Sarah did not wish to take leave of her sister on such a note. "How are the Farwells?"

Her mention of the family where Emma was currently employed as a governess was clearly a poor choice. A telling shudder wracked Emma's slender form. "Unspeakable."

Sarah's hand tightened on Emma's arm in sympathy. "You will always have a home here."

Emma smiled, but gave a faint shake of her head. She had been implacable in her determination to support herself. "I believe I shall seek a post outside London. There is a Lady Hartshore in Kent who is seeking a companion."

Sarah's heart twisted. Emma would have to face her demons in her own manner. "Do not forget to seek out a bit of happiness," she urged. "It is not such a terrible thing."

Emma's pale features abruptly softened, bringing to life her delicate beauty. "I will always have happiness as long as I have you, Sarah." Placing a kiss upon Sarah's cheek, Emma gently pulled free and moved through the door.

With a loving smile, Sarah watched her leave, only turning about as her youngest sister gave a loud snort.

"What a dreary goose she is," Rachel complained.

Sarah's smile was replaced with a stern frown at the flippant accusation. "Emma is very sensitive to our less than respectable circumstances."

"Pooh. She has always been the greatest bore."

"Emma is to be admired for her determination to make her own way in the world," Sarah retorted, her gaze narrowing. "Speaking of which, I have several bills here I wish to discuss with you."

Rachel gave an airy wave of her hand. In true Cresswell fashion, the minx believed she was above such mundane manners as money. It would never occur to her that Sarah and Emma must sacrifice to allow her to live in grand style.

Just for a moment Sarah felt in complete sympathy with Lord Chance. Neither of them had desired to fill the role of a stern taskmaster, and yet both had been thrust into the position by fate. It was not an easy situation.

"Oh, not now, Sarah," Rachel complained. "I have an invitation to dine with the Montfords."

"You always appear to have an invitation when I wish to speak with you."

Rachel smiled with satisfaction. "I am very much in demand."

"Yes." Sarah paused, choosing her words with great care. Although the rumors that had come to her attention deeply alarmed her, she was too wise to goad the impetuous child into even more daring behavior. "Rachel, I hope you will take care."

"Whatever do you mean?"

Sarah's expression was somber. For all the aggravation she endured, she truly was fond of her sister, and she knew that deep down Rachel possessed a kind heart and generous spirit. Only her need for gaiety and adventure led her astray.

"I have no desire for you to do something foolish."

Rachel's tiny chin jutted outward in a familiar

motion. "I only intend to enjoy myself. Why should I not?"

"You possess a habit of rushing into situations with little thought of the consequences," Sarah pointed out gently.

"No doubt you wish me to be as dull and stuffy as Emma."

Sarah gave a slow shake of her head. Could three sisters possibly be more different?

"I wish you to have no regrets."

Rachel's hazel eyes flashed with the same smoldering fire that could be found in the Devilish Dandy. "I have never regretted anything, nor do I intend to begin now." Moving forward, Rachel lightly kissed Sarah's cheek. "Forgive me, I really must run. Tell Father I shall call on him later in the week. Oh . . . do you have a few pounds I could borrow? I saw the most darling muff that I simply must have."

"No," Sarah promptly denied.

Rachel gave a charming laugh. "Very well. Good-bye, dearest, and try not to look so grim. You are so very handsome when you smile."

In a cloud of rose perfume, Rachel swept from the room.

Left on her own, Sarah heaved a sigh. If only her mother had lived beyond Rachel's infancy. Perhaps she would have possessed the knowledge to soothe Emma's troubles and tame Rachel's wild spirits. At least she might have provided a sense of security as their father had dragged them throughout Europe and at last England.

Sarah had done the best she could, aided by Lord Scott, who had been the only person she could depend upon when her father was arrested. But she very much feared it was not enough.

"Excuse me, Miss Cresswell."

Chiding herself for wasting her time on foolish regrets, Sarah turned to view Watts standing in the doorway. "Yes?"

"I thought you would like to know I visited those jewelers you requested."

"Any luck?"

Watts gave a firm shake of his head. "No, and seeing as they know I work for the Devilish Dandy, they wouldn't feel the need to lie. Lud, most would love to crow that someone bested the master."

Sarah could not prevent a small smile. Watts's battered nose was clearly out of joint at the thought of her father losing his claim to being the best thief in London.

"Thank you, Watts."

"There are a few more discreet collectors that your father preferred. I shall seek them out tomorrow."

"What should I do without you?" she asked softly. Then, as the servant blushed in embarrassment, she readily eased his discomfort. "Have you seen Father?"

"Not since breakfast, miss."

Sarah heaved yet another sigh. "I suppose it is too much to hope he is not busily embroiling himself in trouble."

A faintly sympathetic smile touched the brutish features. "As to that, I cannot say."

"You realize, Watts, that I never should have gotten out of my bed yesterday."

"Yes, miss. A most unfortunate occurrence."

Five

Few glancing out their window that November morning would have taken much note of the glossy black carriage that briefly slowed beside a hedge before continuing down the elegant street. Certainly no one could have detected the slender lad swiftly darting through the late morning shadows.

Alone with Miss Cresswell in the carriage, Chance allowed himself to study the slender maiden seated across from him. This morning she had chosen a lovely walking dress and pelisse in dove gray with a band of ermine at the hem and cuffs. Upon her chestnut curls, she had perched a bonnet crowned with pink roses that framed her handsome countenance to advantage.

She might have been just another of the pretty maidens who currently filled the London drawing rooms, but Chance was swiftly realizing Miss Cresswell was far from being just another maiden.

Who else of his acquaintance would have proven to possess such skill or courage? Certainly none would have exhibited the audacity to help him recover the Chance diamonds.

She had proven herself a decided puzzle. And

for a gentleman who prided himself on being a
shrewd judge of his fellow man, such a puzzle
was bound to capture his interest.

That was, of course, why she had been so fre-
quently upon his thoughts, he assured himself,
and why he had awakened this morning with a
distinct sense of anticipation.

When he was in Miss Cresswell's company, he
never knew what might occur next. It was an
oddly exhilarating feeling.

As he allowed his gaze to rise to her pale countenance, a small smile curved his lips. Yes, a puzzle indeed.

The carriage slowed to a halt, and Chance
watched as Miss Cresswell abruptly leaned to
glance out the window at his mother's home.
"Oh . . . it is very grand," she breathed.

It was grand. Of Palladian design, Primrose was
built on stately lines with a stucco finish and brass
railings. Two arched windows were framed by
towering columns, while a sweeping staircase that
boasted two large urns completed the image of
sophistication. The interior was even grander,
with a curved oak staircase and furnishings of satinwood. Few did not discover themselves somewhat overawed by the grandeur.

"Do not fear," he said in soft tones. "My
mother is a very comfortable woman who is anxious to like everyone she encounters."

As he had hoped, the brief unease he had detected in Miss Cresswell was swiftly banished as
she turned to regard him with that sparkling
gaze. "Not at all like her son."

Chance's smile widened. "No, I fear I have
taken after my late father, while Ben was fortu-

nate to inherit my mother's sunny nature—which is no doubt why she dotes upon him."

Unlike most who found Chance's mocking sense of humor disarming, Miss Cresswell merely lifted a chestnut brow. "Does that bother you?"

"Not at all," he retorted with all honesty. "I am very fond of both my mother and brother, although at the moment I would happily wring Ben's neck. Do you have siblings?"

She gave a surprisingly rueful grimace. "Yes. A sister Emma who is currently a governess with the Farwells and Rachel, who is staying with friends in town. And, like you, there are moments when I wish to place my hands about their lovely necks."

Intrigued by the sudden glimpse of the woman beneath the cool exterior, Chance stroked a finger down the length of his jaw. "You are the eldest?"

"Yes."

"It appears that we have much in common."

Their gazes entangled for a long moment of silent understanding. Then, as if realizing she was revealing more than she intended, she briskly straightened her shoulders.

"Lucky should have reached the back of the house. We should go."

Chance's lips twitched, but he readily conceded to her command. With seamless grace, he flowed from the carriage. Then, with equal ease, he promptly turned toward the woman about to step onto the street and swept her into his arms.

"My lord . . ." Miss Cresswell gasped in shock, attempting to pull away from the strength of his chest.

Chance firmly bundled her even closer, rather

startled to discover just how delicious she felt in his arms. He had always chosen delicate, utterly feminine mistresses who deferred to him in all matters. Yet none had felt quite as right as this towering, pertly commanding wench. He inhaled the warm, enticing scent of her as he began to walk toward the wide steps.

"Recall that you have sorely twisted your ankle," he drawled close to her ear.

"I am too large to be carried about," she protested in satisfyingly breathless tones.

His dark gaze studied her heated cheeks. "You are tall, but as slender as a reed."

"My lord, you shall strain your back and put an end to our deception."

"Rest assured, Miss Cresswell, that my back is in no danger." Which was true enough, Chance acknowledged, although he very much feared holding her in such an intimate manner was creating dangers of another sort altogether. "Perhaps you should be concentrating on your role as a damsel in distress."

Her lips thinned at his deliberate words. "I wish you to know it is a role I detest above all others."

He gave a low chuckle. "So I suspected."

Whatever response she might have made was halted as the front door opened to reveal a gaunt butler with a stony countenance that had not betrayed an expression in thirty years. Today was no exception. He merely stepped backward to allow Chance room to carry his unusual burden inside the foyer.

"Franklin, I fear that there has been an accident."

"This way, sir."

No more ruffled than if Chance had arrived with a box of chocolates, Franklin led the way from the foyer up to Lady Chance's private salon.

Entering the long room decorated in ebony with gold leaf, marble walls, and a fine collection of porcelain, Chance swept past his startled mother to gently place Miss Cresswell on an ivory settee.

"Goodness, what has occurred?" Lady Chance demanded.

Allowing his arms to linger longer than strictly necessary, Chance at last straightened to confront the small, silver-haired matron attired in a morning gown of French black bombazine trimmed with white satin.

"I was coming to visit you when I viewed Miss Cresswell trip and twist her ankle."

"So foolish of me," Miss Cresswell properly apologized, a hint of color still staining her cheeks. "I beg your pardon for the intrusion."

As Chance had expected, his mother's kind heart was instantly roused to compassion.

"Nonsense. It is the simplest thing in the world to twist an ankle. Why, I did so last year and was forced to my bed for a week. Franklin, please have Mrs. Bross bring a bowl of hot water. We shall also need the brandy."

The servant offered a creaking bow. "Very good, my lady."

"We shall give that ankle a nice soak," Lady Chance said with a sympathetic smile. "That always makes me feel better."

"You are very kind," Miss Cresswell murmured.

"And I volunteer to rub away any lingering pain," Chance promised with a roguish smile.

"You will do no such thing." His mother emphatically took command of the situation. "Indeed, you will leave us now, Oliver."

"But . . ."

"Now."

Ignoring the sudden widening of Miss Cresswell's lovely eyes, Chance gave a ready bow. "As you insist, Mother. If you would be so good as to have another brandy sent to the library."

"Tea," his mother corrected.

"That seems monstrously unfair if you and Miss Cresswell are allowed to partake of Father's fine cellar."

"It is for medicinal purposes only," his mother informed him primly.

Chance ignored the discreet motion Miss Cresswell was making for him to remain. As delightful as he found the prospect of catching a glimpse of her ankle, he had schemes of his own.

"Of course." With a rather wicked smile toward his partner in crime, he strolled languidly from the room. In the hall, he waited until a flustered Mrs. Bross, with two maids in tow, passed carrying the bowl of hot water and a decanter of brandy. Behind them, the butler maintained an air of dignified composure.

"Franklin." Chance halted the servant as he was about to pass. "May I have a word?"

Stepping into the library, Chance waited for Franklin to enter behind him and shut the door. The room was Chance's favorite at Primrose. Decidedly masculine, with glass cases that housed hundreds of leather-bound books, it had escaped his mother's rather ostentatious style and remained gracefully stark.

Turning to regard the butler, he chose his

words with great care. "I wish to speak with you of the servants."

There was a startled silence. "I beg your pardon?"

"Have you noted anything unusual among the staff?"

"I fear I do not quite comprehend," the servant said in wooden tones.

Hoping to appear as casual as possible, Chance moved to pour himself a glass of his father's favorite sherry.

"Has anyone suddenly quit their position or seemed to acquire a sudden windfall?"

"Certainly not, sir. The staff have all been with Lady Chance for several years," the butler stated without hesitation. "Has something occurred?"

Chance was prepared for the obvious question. "There has been a rumor of several robberies throughout the neighborhood."

There was the faintest thinning of Franklin's lips. "I can assure you that the staff is above suspicion, my lord."

Chance took a lazy sip of his sherry. "No doubt you are right. I, however, would appreciate your keeping your eyes open. Report to me anything unusual. We cannot be too careful in guarding Lady Chance."

"Certainly, sir. Will there be anything else?"

Chance grimaced as he set aside his glass. "Brandy."

"At once."

Bowing, the servant disappeared, and Chance moved to gaze at the coals burning brightly in the grate. He had not expected to learn much from Franklin. He had indeed been more intent on keeping the wily man occupied while Lucky

was searching the servants' quarters. Still, he did
feel somewhat reassured by the knowledge that
there were no overtly suspicious characters
lodged beneath his mother's roof.

Forcing himself to wait for the brandy, Chance
slowly sipped the aged spirit before giving in to
his impatience and returning to the salon.

His entrance could not have been more timely.
Although the bowl of water had been set aside,
the maids were still in the process of pulling the
stocking onto Miss Cresswell's shapely leg. Very
shapely leg, he acknowledged, as his mother gave
a squeak and the heavy skirts were abruptly
dropped to hide the enticing view.

"Really, Oliver, you shall put Miss Cresswell to
the blush."

Chance raised his gaze to meet Sarah's sparkling blue eyes. "That I should very much like
to witness."

Clearly determined to appear indifferent to his
lingering gaze, Miss Cresswell primly folded her
hands in her lap. "Your mother has been telling
me of her Christmas party."

Chance was not at all deceived. However calm
she might pretend to be, there was no hiding
the pink in her cheeks. His mother, thankfully,
was more easily distracted.

"Yes, it is ever so vexing, Oliver," she cried.
"Lady Doland has arranged her own Christmas
Ball the very night before mine. She has always
been quite envious of my success, and I have no
doubt she is spiteful enough to spend her entire
fortune just to outshine me."

With perfect composure, Chance withdrew his
silver snuff box and helped himself to a small

measure. "I am quite certain her efforts will pale
in comparison to your superior skill as a hostess."

His mother regarded him with a knowing expression. "Meaning you haven't the slightest interest in my gathering."

"Would I be so shameless?"

"Yes," she promptly retorted. "Thankfully, Miss
Cresswell is far more considerate. She has suggested several charming notions that will certainly
make Lady Doland's affair seem unbearably insipid."

The faintest hint of alarm pricked at Chance.
Although he had uncharacteristically thrust aside
his concern at bringing the daughter of the Devilish Dandy into his mother's home, he was not
without a few qualms. After all, Miss Cresswell
herself admitted her upbringing was far from traditional.

"Indeed?"

"Oh, yes," Lady Chance happily chattered. "I
shall allow Lady Doland to have her tedious ball
while I shall entertain our guests with charades
and snapdragons and carols . . . What else was
there, my dear?"

"A wassail bowl," Miss Cresswell offered in dry
tones, her expression revealing she had not missed
his momentary suspicion.

"Yes, of course." Lady Chance smiled with anticipation as she inwardly envisioned her elegant
guests' surprise at such festive entertainments.
"And games, of course. It shall be delightful."

"How very fortunate Miss Cresswell happened
to turn her ankle just outside your door," he said
in low tones, his gaze never leaving Miss
Cresswell's stiff countenance.

"A most amazing stroke of fortune," his

mother readily agreed, turning to her savior. "I do wish you would agree to attend, my dear."

Miss Cresswell gave a firm shake of her head. "That is very kind, but I could not possibly."

"You must convince her, Oliver," Lady Chance demanded in tones that revealed her conviction no one could resist his charm.

Chance was not nearly so confident. Thus far Miss Cresswell had proven to be remarkably indifferent to his supposed charms.

"I shall do my best," he murmured, unable to deny a faint disappointment that Miss Cresswell would not be attending. Her presence would certainly provide a welcome diversion from the other insipid maidens. "For now, however, I believe I should return her home."

Moving forward, Chance prepared to once again scoop her into his arms, only to be outmaneuvered as she hastily scrambled to her feet.

"My ankle is much improved."

"Are you quite certain, Miss Cresswell? I should not like you to do yourself injury."

"Quite, quite certain."

"A pity," he murmured lowly.

Taking her arm, he began to escort her across the room when suddenly his rather scatterbrained mother hit upon something odd. "Oliver, why did you come to see me?"

"A trifling business matter," Chance smoothly lied. "I shall call later in the week."

"And you will speak with Miss Cresswell about the party?"

"I shall devote my fullest attention to Miss Cresswell," he readily promised.

Leaving the room, they made their way down the staircase and into the gray weather. The carriage was promptly awaiting them and, first settling Miss Cresswell with a warm blanket, Chance took his own seat before calling out for the groom to set the horses in motion.

Alone again, Chance regarded his companion with a faint smile. "What did you think of my mother?"

"I found her to be surprisingly kind as well as charming."

Effectively implying he was neither kind nor charming, he acknowledged. The shrew.

"Surprising, indeed." An impish glint entered his dark eyes. "Almost as surprising as the decidedly shapely curve of your leg. You know, Miss Cresswell, I did you a disservice to presume that, like most slender females, you would be all bones and skin. Now that I have been allowed such a tantalizing glimpse, I will never gaze upon you quite the same."

Predictably she resorted to no maidenly shrieks or swoons at his devilish teasing. Instead, she favored him with a level gaze. "Tell me, my lord, are you always this annoying, or do you make a special effort for my sake?"

Chance gave a sudden laugh. "Oh, definitely a special effort. I rarely encounter anyone worthy of being annoying to."

"I am flattered," she mocked. Then, as the carriage abruptly halted, she glanced out of the window. "There is Lucky."

The carriage door was pulled open and Lucky bounced in even as the horses were once again urged into motion. Flopping on the seat next to Miss Cresswell, the lad heaved a tragic sigh. "Another bust. Not so much as a hidden quid. That housekeeper must be a real dragon."

Chance couldn't help but be amused at Lucky's patent disgust at such a well-regulated household. "Mrs. Bross is quite efficient," he commiserated.

"No doubt the sort that pokes her nose into every crook and cranny."

"Yes, quite detestable."

"I'd say," Lucky retorted with genuine horror.

Giving a slight shake of her head at their antics, Miss Cresswell turned the conversation to more important matters. "So we have seemingly ruled out the servants at both your brother's and your mother's homes."

"Ah, yes, I almost forgot." Chance reached into his greatcoat to remove a folded slip of paper. He handed it to the curious maiden opposite him. "My brother had this delivered yesterday."

Miss Cresswell skimmed the list of names with a professional eye. "Good."

Chance was again reaching into his pocket to produce a prettily wrapped package. "The maid who brought the note also requested that this trifling gift be given to Samuel."

"Oh." Her firm features promptly flushed with color. "I suppose you think this vastly amusing."

"Not at all." Chance heaved a mocking sigh. "It is rather lowering to consider that your brief charade as a male managed to slay the heart of a modest maiden while the remainder of us gentlemen must struggle for days, perhaps weeks to win the briefest of smiles."

Miss Cresswell's blue eyes sparked with danger. "Sir . . ."

"However, I do hope you write to the poor dear and inform her that her hopes are for naught."

"I shall do no such thing."

"I beg you to reconsider." He regarded her from beneath lowered lids. "Imagine my discomfort at having a lovelorn maiden hovering about my home in the hopes of glimpsing the elusive Samuel. Why, she might go into a decline and expire upon my doorstep. Then where should I be?"

Her lips thinned in annoyance, but before she could speak, the scent of apple tarts drifting from the package overpowered the young urchin.

"Are you going to eat that?" he demanded in hopeful tones.

Miss Cresswell promptly shoved the gift into his ready hands. "Here."

"Are you blushing, Miss Cresswell?" Chance lightly teased.

"No, I am not," she denied. "I am simply cold."

"Allow me." With gentle care, Chance leaned forward to pull the blanket up to her shoulders, lingering to gaze deep into her widened blue eyes. "You smell of lilacs."

A timeless moment passed as Chance allowed his gaze to drop to the satin softness of her lips. What would they taste like beneath his mouth? Would they part in invitation? Would they tremble with innocent fear or ignite with passion?

A crazed, nearly uncontrollable urge to discover the truth had his head bending downward before her soft gasp had him abruptly sitting back in his seat.

Good gads. What was he thinking? He was no clumsy schoolboy to attempt to make love to a maiden in his own carriage—and with Lucky looking on, to boot.

Clearly he was in need of seeking a new mistress.

Maybe several.

"Shall we discuss the names upon the list?" Miss Cresswell asked in uneven tones.

Chance struggled to regain his normal nonchalance. "By all means."

She peered at the list. "May I ask who Fiona is?"

Drat. Chance gave a small cough, his entire body tingling with an unfamiliar heat.

"My brother's . . ."

"Mistress?" she finished with a casualness he could only envy.

"Yes."

"I believe I shall investigate her next. She must have some acquaintances among the courtesans."

His momentary discomfort was banished at her outrageous proposal. "You cannot visit a member of the demimonde."

"I can and I will, my lord," she retorted in firm tones, a hint of cool challenge in her blue eyes. "I quite understand if you prefer to cry off."

His lips snapped together. Whatever insanity had given him the sharp desire to bed this maiden did not diminish his realization that she was, indeed, a lady. He would not allow her to tramp through the dens of iniquity unattended.

The devil take Ben and his foolish behavior, he seethed. By rights he should be the one in this carriage.

The earl dismissed the thought as soon as it entered his head. If anyone was going to the local brothels with Miss Cresswell, it was he.

"I shall call on you first thing in the morning."

Six

The following morning, Sarah attired herself in a heavy wool gown and scraped back her hair in a stern mood. She had deliberately ignored the cabinet filled with satin and jaconet gowns that were far more flattering.

She was a spinster, she reminded herself for the hundredth time since she had fled Lord Chance's carriage. She was far too old, not to mention far too wise, to yearn for the feel of a gentleman's kiss.

Granted, when he had been poised above her in the carriage, her stomach had trembled with a strange excitement. And perhaps her dreams had been troubled by pale, elegant features and mocking black eyes. But it was nothing more than . . . a momentary lapse.

This morning she was once again in firm command. And she possessed the comfort of knowing Lord Chance could not possibly have suspected her brief madness.

And he would never suspect, she assured herself as she crisply headed out of her chambers and down to the front salon.

From today forward she would be calm, rational, and utterly sensible, not at all the sort of maiden to yearn for heated kisses.

With this comforting thought, she swept inside the room, prepared to await Lord Chance's arrival. She had taken only a few steps, however, when she stumbled to a halt at the sight of her father.

Once again, he was flamboyantly attired in a striped crimson coat and knee breeches. And once again he sported that ridiculous eye patch.

Turning from the pier mirror, where he was busily fussing with his cravat, he offered her a roguish smile. "Oh, Sarah, tell me what you think." He minced in a circle to offer her the full effect of his ensemble. "A trifle gaudy perhaps, but precisely what a French rogue would choose, I believe."

Sarah gave a delicate shudder. "It is very bright."

"Festive," the Devilish Dandy corrected. "Precisely what is needed to combat this dreary English weather."

"I believe the weather is particularly fine in India," she said in dry tones.

"As hot as Hades, I should rather think."

Strolling further into the room, she eyed her unpredictable relative with a firm gaze. "May I inquire where you took yourself off to yesterday?"

"But of course." He gave a vague shrug. "As I promised, I was assisting you, my dearest."

Sarah felt a chill of dismay inch down her spine. She had no desire for her father's particular brand of assistance. "What have you done?"

He calmly arranged the lace at his cuffs. "Merely made a few discreet inquiries among those who would be in a position to know if the Chance diamonds were floating about."

She released a tiny sigh. Her father was clearly indifferent to the danger of his position in London. Indeed, she would not put it past him to visit the Prince himself if the urge was to take him. At least he should be safe enough if he remained among those he trusted.

"And are they?" she demanded, knowing that if anyone could discover the truth it was her father.

"No. There has not been so much as a whisper."

Sarah nibbled her bottom lip. "So whoever has taken them has not yet attempted to sell them."

"Not in London," Solomon pointed out. Then, holding out one foot, he studied the pointed shoe. "What of these buckles?"

Sarah shook her head in a rueful fashion. "Ghastly."

"I fear you may be right." He sighed. "Still, they set my stockings off quite nicely."

Sarah was no more fond of the pink stockings than the flashy buckles. "Few gentlemen still wear such attire unless it is a formal affair."

"But I am an elderly, rather eccentric gentleman who prefers the more gracious fashions of days past." That charming smile flashed again. "Besides, it would be a sin to hide such a shapely calf."

The memory of another lethally charming gentleman referring to shapely legs sent a shock of heat through her body. She stiffened in annoyance with herself. "Please, Father, I have heard quite enough of legs in the past two days."

"Really?" His one visible green eye narrowed. "I thought you were with Lord Chance."

Sarah refused to blush. The devil take Lord Chance. "I was."

"And he speaks to you of legs? Perhaps I should have a word with the gentleman. I will not have my daughter treated as a lightskirt."

"You will do no such thing," Sarah retorted in tones that defied argument. "Lord Chance is interested in nothing more than retrieving his mother's diamonds."

"No gentleman is that tediously dull-witted," her father protested.

"No, he is not dull-witted. He is arrogant, interfering, and altogether annoying."

Too late, she realized she had revealed more of her inner disturbance than she had intended. With a practiced motion, Solomon raised his quizzing glass.

"Well, well."

"Do not regard me in that fashion, Father."

"No, no, *enfin.*" He gave a click of his tongue. "Not Father, but Uncle Pierre."

Sarah rolled her eyes at his chastisement. "You do realize that if you encounter a true Frenchman, he will no doubt run you through for torturing his language in such a wretched fashion?"

The quizzing glass dropped as the Devilish Dandy gave an indifferent shrug. "He might make the attempt."

Knowing her father was indeed a master with both a sword and pistols, Sarah allowed his confident boast to stand. "Will you be dining in tonight?"

"I have received an invitation to dine with Mrs. Surton and several other notable guests."

Sarah took a startled step forward. "No."

"Do not fret." Her father gave a chuckle at her obvious dismay. "I have sent a lovely bouquet along with my regrets that I possess a prior engagement. Such a lovely lady."

"She is detestable, as you well know," Sarah retorted in tart tones. No one could ever presume to consider Mrs. Surton as a lovely lady, not even the Devilish Dandy. "But I have need of her for my school. I would appreciate your staying away from her."

"So she can dribble out a pittance and keep you firmly beneath her heel?" A rare hint of annoyance flickered over his lean features. "Nonsense. With a bit of encouragement, I can assure that she provides you a proper sum as well as keep her far too occupied to bother you."

It was, indeed, a tempting thought, she acknowledged, to have the money that was so vital to keep the school open with none of the aggravation of enduring the meddlesome attentions of Mrs. Surton. At the same moment, she realized she could not possibly allow her father to trifle with the older woman's affections. Good heavens, could there be anything worse than having a lovesick Mrs. Surton crying upon her shoulder? The revolting image sent a shudder through her slender frame. "I appreciate the thought, but I would prefer you do not meddle in my affairs."

Solomon gave a pat to his intricate cravat. "But, my dear, I am your father. It is my duty to meddle."

Sarah's expression hardened. "Father."

"Not now, Sarah," the Devilish Dandy pleaded as he strolled toward the door. "I really must be off."

"Where are you going?"

Pausing in the doorway, Solomon smiled with wicked amusement. "Did I not tell you? I am meeting Lord Maxwell. *Au revoir,* my dearest."

The ornate brothel was discreetly set back from the street and nearly hidden by a high hedge.

It was a house Sarah had, shockingly, visited on a number of occasions. Her work with children had often included those offsprings of prostitutes. And as one of the most elegant and renowned brothels in London, it had only been a matter of time before she had arrived on the doorstep to meet with the notorious owner.

In truth, Sarah had been caught off guard by Madame Vallenway, not only by her shrewd intelligence, but by her genuine concern for the women who resided in her brothel. Although Sarah could never condone such a life, she was wise enough to realize the woman could prove a valuable ally in improving the future for the children born within her home.

Since that day, Sarah had regularly visited with trifling gifts and, more importantly, with recommendations for establishing a small school for those children old enough to study.

Of course, as a rule she made her visits with Watts as a companion, she acknowledged with a covert glance at the dark-haired gentleman seated across the carriage. It was bound to be a trifle more awkward with Lord Chance.

With a silent chastisement at her uncharacteristic bout of nerves, Sarah pulled the large basket she had brought with her onto her lap.

Blast those ridiculous dreams. They were making her as silly as a schoolgirl.

Thankfully, Lord Chance had seemed far too distracted to note her odd behavior. Since he had arrived to collect her, there had been a reserve in his manner that had not been present since their initial encounter. She could only presume he was growing impatient with their lack of success in locating the diamonds.

No more impatient than she was, she acknowledged with a inner sigh. Even with all her silent admonishments, she could not deny she was wretchedly conscious of the male cologne filling the carriage and the occasional brush of his knee against her own.

Preparing to alight as the carriage pulled to a halt, Sarah was detained as Lord Chance gave a choked cough. With a flare of surprise, she turned to discover his aloof expression had been replaced with one of dark disapproval. "Good gads, you do not propose to enter such an establishment."

She gave a lift of her shoulder. "Of course."

"Miss Cresswell . . . Sarah . . ." he was provoked to mutter, his dark eyes uncommonly somber. "I will not allow you to expose yourself to such a place, even for the sake of retrieving the diamonds."

Oddly moved by his concern, she conjured a reassuring smile. "You need have no fear, my lord. I will survive quite nicely."

Without giving him an opportunity for further protest, Sarah slipped through the door being held open by the groom. She then set a brisk pace up the pathway to the front steps. Lord Chance had just managed to pull even with her when the door was opened to reveal a stout, decidedly muscular butler.

At the sight of Sarah, the servant abruptly dropped his intimidating scowl to smile with genuine pleasure. "Miss Cresswell, welcome."

"Thank you, Dodwell. Is Madame Vallenway available?"

Dodwell gave a brief, considering glance toward the silent gentleman at Sarah's side before nodding his head. "Of course. This way."

The butler led them through the overly lavish foyer and down a long hall to the back of the vast home. As always, Sarah kept her gaze averted from the shocking statues and paintings that lined the walls. Not until Dodwell had unlocked a heavy door and escorted them into the private quarters did she once again lift her head.

The salon they entered was far more traditional in decor. With solid oak furnishings and framed panels of crimson silk upon the walls, it might have belonged to the most prim hostess in London.

Stepping close beside her, Lord Chance bent to whisper in her ear. "You are acquainted with Madame Vallenway?"

She glanced up to meet his narrowed gaze. "I know many people in London, sir."

Whatever he might have retorted was halted as a magnificent woman rose from a writing desk to cross toward them.

Although no longer in the first blush of youth, Madame Vallenway was still breathtakingly lovely, with a mass of titan curls and dark eyes. It would be a mistake, however, to presume she relied solely on her beauty. There was an iron will and innate cunning beneath the carefully polished image.

"Sarah, dearest." She smiled happily, then turned a coy glance toward the handsome gentleman. "And Lord Chance."

The most absurd prick of annoyance entered her heart at Madame Vallenway's swift recognition of Lord Chance. The toad. Little wonder he was reluctant to enter the brothel.

"I see no introductions are necessary," she said in determinedly even tones.

Perhaps sensing Sarah's sudden tension, Madame Vallenway was swift to distract her young visitor. "Whatever are you doing here?"

Sarah held out her basket. "I have brought you this."

With a fond click of her tongue, Madame Vallenway accepted the basket and set it on a low table. "Sarah. I have told you that you must halt your generosity."

"It is just a few treats for the children."

"Children?" Lord Chance spoke for the first time, his tone one of confusion.

A faint smile curved madame's full lips. "A hazard for women in my profession."

Lord Chance gave a choked noise. Feeling her own surge of embarrassment, Sarah rushed into speech. "Madame ensures that the women are allowed to keep their children with them. She even hired a teacher for the older ones."

A hint of satisfaction could be detected in her lovely features.

"It is my hope they will be given the opportunities that too few are ever given. However, it is a modest effort when compared to dear Sarah's school."

Sarah felt Lord Chance's piercing gaze upon her profile. "Nonsense," she murmured. Then, anxious to bring the rather awkward meeting to a swift end, she came to the point of her visit. "I have a question for you."

"Yes?"

"Are you acquainted with Fiona Snow?"

"Of course." Madame's gaze once again shifted to Lord Chance. "Is she not currently under the protection of your brother?"

Chance cleared his throat. "Quite right."

Madame turned back to Sarah, clearly intrigued. "What do you wish to know?"

"What sort of woman is she?"

"Pretty, of course," Madame readily answered, "but unfortunately a silly widgeon."

"Is she devious?"

The courtesan gave a startled blink. "Good heavens, she hasn't the sense to be devious. Why do you ask?"

Sarah was well aware she had to choose her words with care. The last thing she desired was to stir undue gossip, not only out of fear that it might eventually flutter its way back to Lady Chance's ear, but because she had no wish to frighten the thief into flight, taking the diamonds with him.

"There are . . . belongings missing from Mr. Coltran's home."

Madame shook her head without hesitation. "No, not Fiona."

"How can you be so sure?" Sarah demanded.

A twinkle entered the dark eyes. "In my business, you learn a thing or two about people. Now, Fiona might lie or even cheat if given the opportunity, but she has no nerve for theft. It takes a brassy wench to steal from a gentleman and then lie in his arms as if nothing had occurred."

She sounded so very certain that Sarah chose not to press the issue.

"If she happened to know of the belongings, would she share the information with her acquaintances?"

This time Madame gave the question considerably more thought. "Fiona has only been in town a few months, hardly long enough to develop many acquaintances," she at last retorted. "And in truth, I have not heard her utter anything that was not connected to her latest gown or the ribbons in her hair."

"Does she spend much time here or perhaps with one of the other girls?"

"Since being provided a house, Fiona rarely stirs from her bed," Madame retorted with a wry smile. "She is rather indolent and not at all inclined to make an effort to do much of anything. I've warned her such habits will soon ruin her beauty, but she hasn't the sense to pay me any heed."

"And none of the other girls have called on her lately?"

"Not to my knowledge. Actually, I would be very much surprised if they had. None of them were particularly close to her, and there is always a bit of jealousy when one girl or another is chosen by a handsome young gentleman."

Knowing that Madame would have been the first to notice if Fiona was behaving oddly or had suddenly come into a fortune, Sarah conceded defeat. Unless the chit was far more clever than she pretended, it did not seem she could be involved in theft.

"If you do manage to overhear any gossip among the girls or if Fiona happens to begin acting queerly, would you let me know?"

Although clearly curious, Madame merely nodded her head. "Certainly."

"Thank you. We must go."

Not waiting for the butler, Sarah turned to leave the room. Lord Chance was closely beside her as they moved back down the long hall in silence.

She was lost in thoughts of her next logical step when Lord Chance abruptly reached out to grasp her arm. Coming to a halt, Sarah glanced up at his handsome countenance in surprise.

"What is it?"

His dark gaze moved over her pale features, lingering a heart-stopping moment on her lips before seeking her wide eyes.

"I said when we first met that you were extraordinary. I did not fully comprehend just how extraordinary."

Unhinged as much by the sudden lurch of her heart as by the unexpected compliment, Sarah attempted to conjure a light tone. "Ridiculous. I am no way out of the common—unless you consider the fact I am the daughter of the Devilish Dandy."

His slender nose flared at her words. "You are Miss Sarah Cresswell, and never have I encountered a woman who would behave such as you."

She gave a breathy laugh. "Now that I readily believe."

Without warning, his hands reached up to cup her face. "I would admire them more if they did."

Her heart again gave that disturbing lurch and,

barely aware she was moving, she leaned toward the heat of his body. She might be all that was sensible, but a force beyond her control held her spellbound as his dark head lowered and he claimed her mouth in a demanding kiss.

The world halted as a storm of sensations flooded her body. It was not her first kiss, but the fumbling meeting of lips she had once experienced was seared to an inconsequential mistake beneath the mastery of his mouth. She trembled, her stomach clenching with a sharp ache.

Lord Chance gave a soft moan as her lips willingly parted. His hands stroked the soft skin of her cheeks before trailing down the line of her neck. Sarah was oblivious to all but the feel of his lips and the trailing fire of his fingers. Nothing else mattered but that she discover where these wondrous feelings might lead her.

Of course, it was bound to come to an end. Even as the tip of his tongue sought entrance to her mouth, the unmistakable sound of approaching footsteps brought them sharply to their senses. Pulling away, Sarah pressed a hand to her racing heart.

Insanity, she numbly assured herself. She was clearly and irrevocably going mad.

With great reluctance Sarah lifted her head to meet his disturbing black gaze, rather surprised to discover a dark flush on his noble features.

Was he as shaken as she by the heat that had flared between them? Or simply embarrassed at having momentarily desired the daughter of a jewel thief?

There was no time to inquire even if she possessed the nerve, as a scantily clad female tripped down the stairs. Not surprisingly, her eyes widened at the sight of Sarah and the tall gentleman at her side.

"Lord Chance, how delightful," the cyprian cried. "Are you here to see me?"

A fierce shudder of pain racked through Sarah's body. Was there any cyprian in all of London who was not acquainted with Lord Chance?

Heavens above, she was a fool, she sternly chastised herself. How could she have allowed him such liberties? No, not allowed, she corrected, invited. Why, she had behaved more brazenly than any of the doxies upstairs.

Furious with herself as well as with the man who had stirred to life such unwelcome sensations, Sarah sent Lord Chance an icy glare. "Shall we go? Or would you prefer I have the carriage sent back to fetch you?"

With a decided scowl, he grasped her arm and began hauling her toward the door. "Good gads, let us go."

Sarah was tugged through the door and down the path at a crisp pace before she angrily wrenched her arm free. "I am perfectly capable of walking on my own, sir."

"I do not . . . know that woman," he muttered in low tones.

Sarah battled the impulsive flare of happiness at his confession. What if he had not enjoyed the favors of the pretty courtesan? It in no way diminished her own reprehensible behavior. "It is really none of my concern, Lord Chance."

His dark eyes suddenly smoldered in an alarming manner. "If we were not in such a public setting I should prove it is very much your concern," he rasped in a tone that sent a quiver down her spine. "But for now I believe I should escort you home so I can go to my club and drink away all thoughts of missing diamonds, brothels, and lips that could drive a man to distraction."

Seven

True to his word, Chance did indeed spend the better part of his evening at his club. Also true to his word, he consumed an admirable amount of brandy in a valiant attempt to forget the disturbing day.

Predictably, the brandy did nothing more than cause his head to pound, and the memories of the day haunted him far into the night.

In peculiar detail, he had recalled the pleasure of holding Miss Cresswell in his arms—the feel of her slender form, the scent of her skin, the willing softness of her lips, and the fierce heat that had raced through his blood as he had at last kissed her.

That kiss . . .

Chance was no innocent. He had enjoyed the pleasures of mistresses, most of them as beautiful as they were experienced. And while he considered his time devoted to them as pleasurable, they certainly had not troubled his thoughts when they were not near. And not one had ever made his heart shudder to a halt with the merest touch of her lips.

It was absurd, he decided as he rose from his

bed and attired himself in a jade coat and fawn breeches. Miss Cresswell was handsome enough, but not the delicate beauty he preferred. And while her swift intelligence and generous nature might inspire his admiration, she possessed none of the allurements necessary to attract a gentleman of discretion.

So why, then, did he long to gather her into his arms and kiss her insensible?

Insanity was the only explanation.

Miss Cresswell might not be socially acceptable, but she was a lady nevertheless, he was forced to remind himself. A lady who would no doubt box his ears if he so much as hinted he would be willing to take her as a mistress.

His unexpected passions would have to be sternly dismissed.

Well, perhaps not entirely dismissed, a renegade voice whispered in the back of his mind.

Surely a stolen kiss or two would not be entirely scandalous. After all, their acquaintance was destined to end at Christmas, one way or another. It would be a sin not to indulge in an occasional temptation.

For once ignoring the crate awaiting him in the library, Chance partook of a light breakfast and called for his carriage. He wished to speak with Miss Cresswell before her sense of respectability managed to convince her he was beyond the pale.

He had just stepped out of the door, however, when a lad hastily ran up the steps to press a note into his hands. With raised brows, he read the crisp words that warned him Miss Cresswell would be unavailable due to her commitment to her school.

Chance hesitated only a moment before entering his carriage and directing his groom to Miss Cresswell's establishment, where he was firmly determined to discover the location of the mysterious school.

In all, it took over an hour before Chance entered the sturdy building situated in an astonishingly horrid neighborhood. He wrinkled his fastidious nose at the garbage littering the streets and the coarse laughter floating from a nearby gin house. Trust Miss Cresswell to plant herself in the seediest street in London, he ruefully acknowledged. He could only pray she possessed the sense to bring Watts when she visited the school.

Thrusting open the door, Lord Chance stepped inside and halted in amazement.

In shocking contrast to the neighborhood, the school was pristinely clean and the few rooms he could see were filled with children busily setting about the task of learning. Even the pervading stench was thankfully overwhelmed by the tempting aroma of baking bread—a decided haven for children forced to live in such wretched poverty.

Any disapproval at Miss Cresswell's exposing herself to such an environment was readily swept aside at the realization of what she was accomplishing. Perhaps there would be those who would condemn a young maiden for exposing herself to such an environment, but Chance felt nothing but a stab of amazed appreciation.

A most extraordinary lady, indeed.

A familiar, sharp-faced urchin stepped into the hall, distracting Chance's thoughts.

"Hello, guv," Lucky greeted with his usual lack of awe at being confronted by a noble.

"Lucky."

A mischievous smile tugged at the boy's lips. "Taken a fancy for orphans, have you?"

"Brat." Chance chuckled. "Where is Miss Cresswell?"

"This way."

With swift movements, Lucky was moving down the hall, and Chance discovered himself forced to hurry to keep pace. They passed through a classroom of children practicing their alphabet before Lucky opened a door to reveal Miss Cresswell seated upon a chair, several children at her feet listening to her tale of Queen Elizabeth. For a moment he merely studied her in silence. Although she was attired in a plain gray gown with only the brilliant sapphire necklace to relieve the severity, she had never appeared lovelier.

Then, as if sensing his presence, her head abruptly lifted and she stiffened in surprise. An odd pang flared through his heart at the knowledge she was less than pleased at his presence.

"My lord."

Chance performed a graceful bow. "Miss Cresswell."

"What . . . what are you doing here?"

"I came to see you."

"Did you not receive my message?"

"I received it," he admitted. "And easily surmised your reason for sending it."

The color abruptly deepened as she rose to her feet. "Perhaps we should speak in my office."

"If you wish."

Ignoring Lucky's speculative gaze, Chance followed Miss Cresswell's stiff form through the room and into a cramped chamber nearly overwhelmed by a massive desk. Firmly closing the door behind him, Chance regarded the maiden, who was doing her best to maneuver a discreet distance between them despite the lack of space.

At last realizing that short of climbing upon the desk she had no recourse but to endure their intimate proximity, Miss Cresswell lifted her head to regard him in a wary manner. "What do you want?"

Chance slowly smiled, inhaling the sweet scent of her skin. "The children appear to be very fond of you."

She blinked in surprise at his unexpected words. "Children are prepared to be fond of anyone who offers them kindness," she informed him in low tones.

"You offer them more than kindness."

"Not only me. There are many involved in the school."

"But I have no doubt you are the force that makes it possible," he said with quiet conviction.

Clearly embarrassed by his praise, she hastily attempted to distract his attention. "Why did you wish to see me?"

Chance allowed his lids to lower, well aware that the next few moments were destined to be difficult. The passion stirring between them had frightened her. Now he had to find some means of reassuring her he meant no harm. "You have struck me as a remarkably intelligent young woman," he softly drawled. "I believe you can deduce my reason for seeking you out today."

Her blue eyes darkened, but she managed to face him with admirable composure. "If you are referring to yesterday, then I must warn you that I have no desire to discuss the . . . our . . ."

"Kiss?" he helpfully supplied.

"Yes."

He lifted a dark brow. "We can hardly pretend it did not occur."

She unconsciously wetted her lips, making Chance's muscles stir in the most unexpected fashion. Good gads, he was in worse condition than he had thought.

"I do not see why," she muttered.

"Perhaps because I do not wish to pretend it did not occur."

She predictably stiffened at his blunt honesty, her eyes widening. "My lord, as you said, I am an intelligent woman. Far too intelligent to be charmed by a practiced rogue."

A practiced rogue. Chance gave an abrupt frown at the insult. He might have accepted the occasional lures of those females who desired a liaison, but he was no rake. Indeed, he had always been excessively careful to avoid susceptible maidens. "You believe I desire to trifle with you?"

She met his gaze squarely. "Do you not?"

Chance was not certain what he desired, beyond the impossible, but he was confident he would never intentionally hurt her. "I will not insult you with lies," he informed her as he took a step closer. Close enough to feel a fine tremor run through her body. "I do find you remarkably attractive and, given the opportunity, I would not hesitate to kiss you again."

"Sir . . ."

He lifted a finger to press it to her lips. "And I believe you did not find our kiss entirely repulsive."

She shook her head in denial. "It was wrong."

He gave a rueful grimace, wishing he could crush her into his arms and prove just how very right it could be. Instead he forced himself to give a shrug. "I assure you I am no rogue attempting to seduce every maiden I encounter. Indeed, it caught me off guard as much as you."

Far from comforted, she brushed aside his lingering finger with a determined hand. "I will become no man's mistress."

He gazed deep into her troubled eyes. "I did not believe for a moment you would."

"No?"

"No," he said firmly. "Although I will admit that while I have rarely been acquainted with a maiden who would attire herself as a servant, keep a young boy within her household who her father had won in a card game, and consort with cyprians, I have never doubted you were a lady."

She searched his countenance for a long moment before her rigid expression abruptly softened.

"Thank you."

There was no mistaking the genuine sincerity in her tone, and Chance felt a momentary pang at the knowledge that a disreputable part of him wished she were not quite such a lady. He swiftly dismissed the unworthy thought, however. He had never pretended to be without fault, no matter what his ridiculous title. "I kissed you, Miss Cresswell, because I could no longer resist temptation, not because I assumed you would be willing to become my mistress."

He heard her breath catch in her throat. "It must never happen again."

"That I cannot promise."

"My lord . . ."

"I will, however, attempt to resist temptation." He overrode her protest.

There was a strained silence as she regarded
him with a wary expression. "I believe you must
be jesting with me."

His smile was self-derisive. "I most fervently
wish I were. However, I believe we have said all
that is to be said on the subject. Have you considered what is to be done next in regards to the
diamonds?"

Caught off guard by the abrupt change in conversation, she took a moment to respond.

"I fear I have not."

"Not to worry. I shall seek out my brother's
club and have a word with his friends." His hand
reached up to stroke a stray chestnut curl. "Do
not fret, Miss Cresswell. All will be well."

Although it was still early, Chance discovered
his brother's club already filled with brilliantly attired dandies. Most were settled around the card
tables, but a brief glance was enough to assure
him that at least two of the gentlemen he sought
were settled beside a window drinking heavily
from a decanter of brandy.

At his entrance, a small gentleman attired in
black rushed to greet him.

"Sir . . . welcome."

"Thank you." Chance allowed the proprietor
to relieve him of his coat and hat.

"May I offer you a refreshment?"

"Perhaps later."

"Such an honor, my lord." The man gave a
deep bow, clearly delighted at having a Corin-
thian grace his establishment.

With a casual stroll, Chance weaved his way

past the ogling bucks until he at last stood beside the table of Fritz and Moreland.

Like his brother, the two were in their early twenties and dressed in the outrageous fashion of Tulips. Unfortunately, neither possessed Ben's slender physique, nor his charming good looks. As a result, they merely appeared absurd in their bright clothing and layers of fobs and braiding. Even worse, there was a vacuous expression upon their round countenances that revealed they possessed little thought beyond their own pleasure.

At his approach, the two dandies struggled to their feet to perform a startled bow.

"May I?" Chance drawled, indicating the remaining chair at the table.

"Oh . . . certainly, certainly," Moreland stammered.

Taking his seat, he regarded his startled companions with his familiar aloof manner. "Have I missed my brother?"

"No, sir, haven't seen him these past days." Fritz's brow furrowed as he performed the difficult task of thinking. "Devilish queer. He ain't poorly, is he?"

Chance did not doubt that his brother was suffering from nothing more than a healthy dose of guilt. "Not to my knowledge."

"Come to think of it, haven't seen Goldie, neither," Moreland piped in.

Fritz gave a loud snort. "No wonder in that. Badly dipped, you know."

"Who ain't?" Moreland sighed.

"Lord, that's true enough." Fritz took a swig of his brandy, seeming to have forgotten his illustrious guest as the two commiserated over the evils of insufficient funds. "Had to call on Grandmother yesterday for a bit of the ready. Gads, you never seen such a fuss over a few hundred pounds."

Moreland shuddered in sympathy, while Chance leaned back in his chair with cool indifference. In truth, he was attending with sharp intensity, carefully taking note of every word and expression.

"Better to face the vultures than a clutch-fisted grandmother," Moreland proclaimed.

Fritz suddenly offered his companion a sly smile. "Or become engaged to the daughter of a wealthy cit."

Moreland blushed, and Chance regarded him from beneath lowered lids.

"Are congratulations in order?"

Moreland flushed even brighter, giving an uncomfortable cough. "Yes, sir. Miss Sindall. Just announced this week."

"Devilishly deep in the pocket," Fritz chimed in.

"How fortunate," Chance murmured.

Chance inwardly sighed. It appeared neither could have been involved with the disappearance of the diamonds. After all, Fritz would never have braved an interview with his notably sharp-tongued grandmother, and Moreland certainly would not be contemplating marriage to a cit if they possessed such expensive trinkets. Besides, it had taken only a few moments to realize neither possessed the intelligence to dissemble. Had they stolen the jewels, they would have been blubbering the truth the moment he had approached.

He gave a faint shake of his head. Would the truth ever be discovered?

"Chance?"

The surprised call of his name had Chance

slowly rising to his feet and turning to discover
Lord Scott regarding him through his raised quizzing glass.

A tall, rather distinguished gentleman with silver
hair and a square countenance, he had been a
close friend of the previous earl. He had generously offered the same friendship to Chance after
his father's death. It was a friendship Chance cher-
ished.

"Lord Scott."

"Whatever are you doing here?" the older gentleman demanded, well aware of Chance's pref-
erence for White's.

Knowing the two fribbles were watching him
with great interest, Chance gave a small shrug.
"Seeking Ben, although it appears that I am out
of luck."

"Join me for a drink?"

Certain he had learned all there was to learn
from Fritz and Moreland, he readily quit their
company with a faint bow. He could not imagine
how Ben endured such twittering fools.

Following Lord Scott to a table in the corner,
he took a seat opposite his friend. Lord Scott
leaned slightly forward, his expression somber.
"How do you go on?"

Ensuring they could not be overheard, Chance
gave a wry grimace. "We have discovered nothing
as yet."

"Have faith in Miss Cresswell," Lord Scott advised with a faint smile. "If anyone can find those
diamonds, it is she."

Chance did not miss the hint of affection in
the older man's tone, and a stab of unreasonable
jealousy twisted his stomach. Although he had
originally suspected Miss Cresswell and Lord

Scott were more than passing acquaintances, he had dismissed his niggling doubts. He could not believe she would be involved with any gentleman, let alone one twice her age. Now he suddenly wondered if her delightful innocence was nothing more than a sham. She was, after all, born to a master of deception. And there was the lingering question of how she could afford a house of her own and elegant clothes to wear.

Feeling a flare of distaste at his doubt, Chance was nevertheless unable to prevent himself from seeking the truth. "Have you known Miss Cresswell for long?" he demanded with what he hoped was a casual manner.

"For many years. She is quite the finest lady of my acquaintance."

"Yes." Chance ran a finger down the length of his jaw. "How did you meet her?"

Lord Scott leaned back at the sudden question, and Chance fancied his expression became somewhat guarded. "Does it matter?"

Chance was not prepared to admit even to himself how much it mattered. "I find it odd that you would be acquainted with the daughter of the Devilish Dandy."

Far too wily to be easily trapped, Lord Scott lifted one shoulder. "I am a great admirer of the work Miss Cresswell performs with children."

"And that is all?"

The pale blue eyes abruptly narrowed. "Are you attempting to discover if my relationship with Miss Cresswell is of an intimate nature?"

Chance knew he should laugh and deny any interest in Miss Cresswell's personal connections. It was certainly none of his concern. But a devil deep inside him refused to allow him to halt. "Is it?"

The square face hardened in a dangerous manner. "Surely that is a matter between Miss Cresswell and myself."

"Are you refusing to tell me?"

With a concise movement, Lord Scott leaned forward until his arms rested upon the table. There was no mistaking the warning glitter in the blue gaze. "I consider Miss Cresswell much as I would a daughter," he said in stern tones. "And I must warn you I would take great offense to anyone who has offered her an insult."

A mixture of emotions flooded through his body—relief that Lord Scott was clearly no more than a father figure to Miss Cresswell and shame that he had allowed himself to misjudge her, if only for a moment. And surprisingly a swift twinge of anger that Lord Scott's fatherly concern had not extended to ensuring Miss Cresswell did not regularly place herself in considerable danger.

"As would I," he said with soft emphasis. "However, I do feel your care for Miss Cresswell has been woefully inadequate."

Lord Scott raised his brows at the abrupt attack. "Really?"

"You are aware that she possesses an urchin her father won in a card game and regularly consorts with Madame Vallenway?"

A disturbingly speculative gleam entered Lord Scott's eyes. "You do not know Miss Cresswell very well if you suppose anything I might have to say would have the slightest influence upon her."

"She is damnably stubborn," Chance was forced to concede.

"Besides, her heart is always in the right place."

Chance was far from satisfied at the flippant response. Really, he expected more from his friend. "That will not protect her from the dangers she deliberately courts, nor prevent her from scandal," he pointed out in clipped tones.

The silver brows lifted even higher. "Watts ensures she is adequately protected, and her father has seen to it she will always be plagued with scandal."

He spoke nothing but the truth, but Chance felt he had been slapped in the face. Her father. No matter how unfair, he could not deny that the Devilish Dandy's legacy would haunt Miss Cresswell for eternity, a legacy that would ensure the doors of Society would remain forever shut.

"Yes," he breathed.

He barely noticed as Lord Scott rose to his feet and rounded the table. "You will let me know if I can be of further service?" the older man requested.

"Yes, thank you," Chance agreed in distracted tones.

Lord Scott dropped a hand upon Chance's shoulder. "Do not judge Miss Cresswell too harshly. She is simply determined to make life better for those in need."

Chance abruptly lifted his gaze. "But who is to make life better for her?"

Lord Scott gave a slow shake of his head. "That question is out of my hands."

With a last pat, Lord Scott moved away, leaving behind a strangely disturbed Chance.

He was uncertain why he should care if Miss

Cresswell was destined to become a spinster, or perhaps eventually marry some coarse laborer. After all, she would soon be out of his life. What her future might hold would be meaningless to him.

Despite his reassuring thoughts, a dark scowl continued to mar his handsome countenance. Only with considerable reluctance did the proprietor force himself to approach the table.

"My lord, may I offer you some brandy?"

Chance abruptly shuddered. Another thick head was the last thing he needed. "Good gads, no."

Eight

Sarah tossed aside her quill with a rare display of annoyance.

She should have finished with her household accounts an hour ago. They were hardly difficult or complicated. But while she had added the columns of her ledger on a half a dozen occasions, she had yet to arrive at the same sum.

It was, of course, entirely Lord Chance's fault.

Although he had been called from London over a week ago, his absence had not put an end to her building sense of restlessness.

Why had he kissed her?

Until that moment, she had been utterly content with her existence. She had even been convinced she was one of those rare women who had no need for a gentleman in her life.

But the sensations Lord Chance had stirred to life had disrupted her smug contentment.

Why had no one warned her of the power of a mere kiss? Her father had taught her to detect a fake work of art at a glance, to cheat at cards and dice, to barter like a clutch-fisted housekeeper, and to carry herself as a lady. He had warned her of all types of pitfalls that loomed for a maiden on her own in London, but never once had he indicated that her greatest danger lay within.

Blast it all.

She had wasted enough hours brooding upon her odd dissatisfaction. She was a lady and, as such, she could not yearn for the kisses of a gentleman far beyond her reach. It would be best if she forgot all about her ridiculous fancies and concentrated instead on finding the Chance diamonds. Once they were located, Lord Chance would be gone from her life and she could return to her pleasant, uneventful existence.

Gritting her teeth in determination, Sarah grasped her quill and determinedly set about paying her stack of bills and tallying her remaining funds.

She had just managed to add the sums correctly when a faint noise had her lifting her head.

Her breath caught at the sight of Lord Chance.

Attired in a deep gold coat and fawn breeches, he appeared strikingly handsome. But it was the glitter of intelligence in his dark eyes and the unshakable character etched into his elegant features that caused Sarah's heart to jump.

If only . . .

No. With a firm movement she rose to her feet. She was no impressionable chit. She was a mature woman, despite the ridiculous manner in which her heart was pounding.

"Miss Cresswell," he said, bowing gracefully.

"My lord." She was relieved to discover her voice came out quite naturally. "I thought you had quit London."

"I had, but I returned as swiftly as possible."

"May I offer you a drink?"

A dry smile suddenly curved his lips. "No, thank you. I prefer to keep my valuables intact."

His teasing reference to her theft of his stickpin went a long way to relieving her sense of unease, and it was with her usual calm manner that she met his glittering gaze. "I only did that because you were behaving in an insufferably smug manner."

He deliberately assumed that lazy nonchalance which so annoyed her. "My manners are always impeccable."

She refused to consider that on at least one occasion his manners had been far from impeccable. Instead she sent him a wry glance. "Is there a reason you called?"

He strolled further into the room, his powerful presence filling the air. "I wish you to know I have spoken with Ben's friends and I am fairly confident they have no connection with the disappearance of the diamonds."

Sarah's brows abruptly lowered into a frown. She did not like being outwitted.

"There is something we are missing," she muttered, unable to pinpoint the elusive sense she had overlooked a vital clue. "Something . . . I must speak with your brother."

Lord Chance gave a faint grimace at her sudden request. "I thought he had fled to Brighton, which is where I have been. He was nowhere to be found. Knowing Ben, however, it will not be long before his bout of guilt has passed and he returns from God knows where to his pleasures in London."

Sarah felt a stab of annoyance toward the irresponsible Ben. He clearly expected his brother to solve all his troubles while he cowered in hid-

We'd Like to Invite You to Subscribe to Zebra's Regency Romance Book Club and Give You a Gift of 4 Free Books as Your Introduction! (Worth $19.96!)

If you're a Regency lover, imagine the joy of getting 4 FREE Zebra Regency Romances and then the chance to have the lovely stories delivered to your home each month at the lowest price available! Well, that's our offer to you and here how you benefit by becoming a Regency Romance subscriber:

- 4 FREE Introductory Regency Romances are delivered to your doorste
- 4 BRAND NEW Regencies are then delivered each month (usually before they're available in bookstores)
- Subscribers save almost $4.00 every month
- You also receive a FREE monthly newsletter, which features author profiles, discounts, subscriber benefits, book previews and more
- No risks or obligations...in other words, you can cancel whenever you wish with no questions asked

Join the thousands of readers who enjoy the savings and convenience offered to Regency Romance subscribers. After your initial introductory shipment, you receive 4 brand-new Zebra Regency Romances each month to examine for 10 days. Then, if you decide to keep the books, you'll pay the preferred subscriber's price.

It's a no-lose proposition, so return the FREE BOOK CERTIFICATE today!

Say Yes to 4 Free Books!
Complete and return the order card to receive this $19.96 value, *ABSOLUTELY FREE!*

If the certificate is missing below, write to:
Regency Romance Book Club
P.O. Box 5214, Clifton, New Jersey 07015-5214
or call TOLL-FREE 1-888-345-BOOK

Visit our website at www.kensingtonbooks.com.

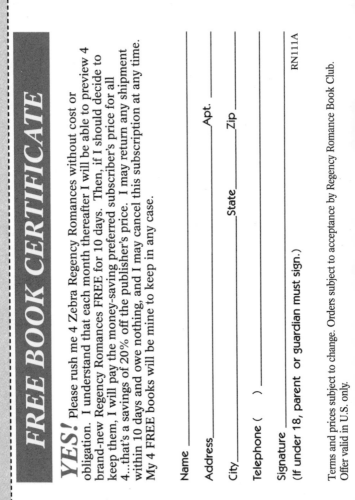

FREE BOOK CERTIFICATE

YES! Please rush me 4 Zebra Regency Romances without cost or obligation. I understand that each month thereafter I will be able to preview 4 brand-new Regency Romances FREE for 10 days. Then, if I should decide to keep them, I will pay the money-saving preferred subscriber's price for all 4...that's a savings of 20% off the publisher's price. I may return any shipment within 10 days and owe nothing, and I may cancel this subscription at any time. My 4 FREE books will be mine to keep in any case.

Name _____

Address _____ Apt. _____

City _____ State _____ Zip _____

Telephone ( ) _____

Signature _____ RN111A
(If under 18, parent or guardian must sign.)

Terms and prices subject to change. Orders subject to acceptance by Regency Romance Book Club.
Offer valid in U.S. only.

Treat yourself to 4 FREE Regency Romances!

A
$19.96
VALUE...
FREE!

No
obligation
to buy
anything,
ever!

ll..l..lll....lll.l.l.l.l.l.l.l.l.ll.l..ll.l.l.ll.l..lll..l

REGENCY ROMANCE BOOK CLUB
Zebra Home Subscription Service, Inc.
P.O. Box 5214
Clifton NJ 07015-5214

ing. It was almost impossible to believe the two could be remotely related. Certainly Lord Chance would never thrust his sins onto another and simply flee.

"This is all most vexing."

His hint of amusement deepened. "Yes, indeed."

With an effort, Sarah realized it was time to swallow her pride.

"Perhaps you should consider contacting the runners."

He gave a slow shake of his head. "I would prefer to keep this quiet a few more days."

"But I fear my boast was sadly misplaced," she forced herself to concede.

Expecting a teasing remark, Sarah was caught off guard as his hand reached up to gently cup her chin.

"Absurd. I have not lost my faith in your skills," he said softly. Then his gaze slowly lowered to the soft curve of her mouth. "Such tempting lips," he murmured, almost as if he were unaware he was speaking aloud. "They have haunted me from London to Brighton and back again."

That quivering pleasure she had battled to quell burst through her lower stomach, making her knees oddly weak. "My lord . . ." she attempted to protest, only to be overrode by a drawling voice behind them.

"Mon Dieu, what have we here?"

Jerking back as if he had been burned, Lord Chance whirled about, giving Sarah full view of her father.

The Devilish Dandy raised his quizzing glass to his one exposed eye to better regard Sarah and Lord Chance. Although there was nothing in his expression to indicate his disapproval, Sarah was not fooled. Solomon might not have been a traditional father, but he would swiftly punish anyone he suspected of trifling with his daughter—more than likely with the point of his sword.

Sarah stepped forward, determined to prevent the brewing trouble.

"Uncle Pierre."

The quizzing glass dropped as Solomon strolled forward. Once again he had chosen a painfully striped coat and knee breeches, and his hair was pulled back with a velvet ribbon.

"It appears my arrival was not a moment too soon."

Refusing to blush, Sarah attempted to play her role as hostess. "Uncle Pierre, may I introduce Lord Chance? Lord Chance, my uncle, Monsieur Valmere."

The earl's dark eyes narrowed. "Monsieur Valmere."

"Uncle Pierre recently arrived from Paris," she hastily added.

Lord Chance's expression was unreadable. "How fortunate."

"Yes." Solomon deliberately allowed his gaze to take inventory of Lord Chance's broad frame before returning to his coolly aloof countenance. "From my understanding, you have become a regular visitor to this household."

Lord Chance folded his arms across the width of his chest. "I hope you are finding London to your liking," he said in soft tones.

Solomon shrugged. "Tolerably."

Hoping to end the encounter as swiftly as possible, Sarah sent her father a warning frown. Lord Chance was too clever to be fooled for long. "Was there something you needed?"

The tension eased somewhat as a satisfied smile touched her father's lips. "I thought you would wish to know of my success at the gaming tables last evening. A most profitable night, indeed."

Sarah felt a chill of fear. Surely her father was not up to his old tricks so swiftly? "You have my congratulations," she said in stiff tones.

He gave a vague wave of his hand. "No, no. No congratulations. It was not my skill that provided my victory. The English gentlemen possess so little finesse, so little patience. And the way they allow brandy to cloud their wits . . . it is incomprehensible."

The thick French accent was absurd, but Lord Chance seemed to discover little amusing about the flowery speech. "I am sorry you found so little sport."

"I do not complain." Solomon removed his snuff box and measured a pinch. "If Lord Maxwell wishes to squander his fortune in such a reckless fashion, I would be most ungracious to refuse his notes."

Sarah's fear swiftly altered to admiration at her father's cunning.

Belatedly she felt Lord Chance stiffen at her side.

"Lord Maxwell?" he demanded.

"Yes, a most . . . how do you English say . . . ill-natured reprobate." The older gentleman replaced his jeweled box. "Still, he did appear quite shaken when he realized just how much money he had lost. His countenance was a most unflattering shade as he confessed it would be next week before he could discharge his debt."

Although thoroughly conscious of Lord Chance's piercing regard, Sarah forced herself to concentrate on her father's words. It had been inordinately clever of him to maneuver Lord Maxwell into such a position. "Which means he shall soon be in need of a large amount of cash," she murmured.

The Devilish Dandy smiled. "My thoughts precisely."

"It appears I am in you debt," Lord Chance said abruptly, proving he was not indifferent to the significance of the notes the older gentleman held.

Solomon stabbed him with a steady glance. "Yes."

Feeling the prickly tension returning, Sarah gave a small cough. "I fear Uncle Pierre demanded an explanation for your numerous visits," she explained hastily.

The two gentlemen seemed to regard each other as prizefighters preparing for a bout.

"With her father gone, I have taken it upon myself to fill the position." Solomon smiled, but there was little humor to it.

Lord Chance remained impervious to the obvious warning. Indeed, a glint of amusement entered the dark eyes. "Oddly enough, Lord Scott informed me of much the same thing."

"Scott." Solomon gave a comical grimace. Not surprisingly, the two gentlemen had always detested one another. "A gentleman of good intentions, but no match for my Sarah."

"No," Lord Chance drawled, turning to regard her with a mocking gaze. "Only a gentleman of remarkable fortitude could hope to keep the reins firmly in check."

Her father possessed the audacity to give a sudden chuckle, as if pleased by the outlandish remark. "You are very perceptive," he complimented.

Sarah thinned her lips. "For your information, I do not appreciate being likened to a horse in need of firm reins," she informed Lord Chance tartly, then turned to regard her father in a stern manner. "You will discover if Lord Maxwell seeks a means of raising the necessary funds?"

He offered her a slight bow. "But of course. Now I am off for bed." He deliberately paused. "Watts, however, shall be just outside the door."

With his less than subtle warning delivered, the Devilish Dandy turned to leave the room. Sarah breathed a sigh of relief, even though it meant she was once again alone with Lord Chance. The less time the two gentlemen spent together the better.

As if emphasizing the danger of the accidental meeting, Lord Chance slowly turned to regard her with an unwavering gaze. "A most unusual gentleman."

She forced herself not to fidget beneath the piercing regard. "Uncle Pierre takes great delight in being unusual."

"You resemble him a great deal."

Blast those all-seeing eyes.

"Perhaps a bit," she hedged. "We are, after all, related."

A silence fell as he studied her determinedly bland expression. Then, quite unexpectedly, he gave a low chuckle. "All but the lips," he softly teased. "Those are uniquely your own."

She sucked in a sharp breath, wondering how she had ever considered herself a calm, unflappable maiden. Lord Chance somehow managed to make her as scatterbrained as Rachel. "My lord, please refrain from discussing my lips." She attempted to sound firm, only to end up sounding breathless.

He stepped closer, filling the air with the scent of warm skin. "Then shall we discuss the delightful shape of your legs?"

"No."

His hand raised as if once again to touch her face, only to abruptly drop as he shook his head. "Perhaps it is a good thing your . . . uncle is in residence," he murmured with a rueful smile. "Do you know I once considered myself quite above such foolishness?"

She frowned warily. "What foolishness?"

He waved aside her question, clearly not prepared to explain his enigmatic words. "I should be leaving. Oh . . ." He appeared to have been struck with a sudden thought. "I almost forgot to tell you that my mother wishes you to visit her tomorrow."

Sarah stepped back in horror. "What?"

He appeared remarkably indifferent. "Some silly nonsense about writing the charades for her Christmas party."

"I cannot visit your mother."

He shrugged, a smile playing about his mouth. "Very well, but be prepared to have her descend upon you here. My mother is very tenacious once she takes a notion into her head, and she is currently convinced that the very success of her gathering hinges upon your contribution."

Have Lady Chance visit her here? Perhaps even encounter the Devilish Dandy? It was not to be thought of.

"You must do something."

He lifted his hands in a helpless motion. "I am no match for a determined hostess."

She could not conceive what he found humorous in the situation, unless he did not fully comprehend the significance of such a visit. "My lord, think of the scandal if it becomes known I have been in your mother's home."

"Who is to know?"

Really, for a sophisticated gentleman he was being extraordinarily dense. Did he not care about his mother's reputation? "The servants at the very least," she pointed out tartly.

"A brief visit by an unassuming miss is hardly the sort of thing to shock the natives," he perversely argued. "Besides, I can see no way out of it."

Her eyes narrowed in exasperation. "You could if you wished to."

He gave a wicked chuckle. "Ah, but you have just sternly stated you do not wish to have your . . . er . . . reins in any way tampered with. I would not dream of interfering."

Sarah was unaccustomed to having her words so efficiently tossed back in her face. Lord Chance might be the most disturbingly attractive gentleman she had ever encountered, but that did not halt him from being the most aggravating as well. "Very well then, I will call on your mother. And when the gossip begins it will be upon your head."

Far from horrified, Lord Chance's grin merely widened. "I shall contrive to bear the scandal."

At promptly eleven o'clock, well before most visitors would be arriving, Sarah presented herself on Lady Chance's doorstep. It had been a dreadful walk across London. Not only had it been a great distance, but the sharp wind had easily cut through her cloak, and the endless puddles had soaked her feet.

She could, of course, have hired a hack. It had, indeed, been her first inclination. But the realization that in this particular neighborhood such a vehicle would attract more than one pair of inquisitive eyes had halted the impulse.

Not that it wouldn't have served Lord Chance right, she seethed. After all, he could easily have fobbed off Lady Chance. His indifference to his mother's delicate reputation was reproachful.

Quite reproachful.

She had repeated those stern words throughout her long walk. Absurdly, it was either that or allow the perfectly ludicrous notion that he did not find her so utterly sunk in scandal to blossom to life. Stamping her feet to attempt to bring life to her frozen toes, she sighed in relief as the butler smoothly pulled open the door.

"Miss Cresswell."

After taking her bonnet and cloak, the servant led Sarah through the vast home to a private salon. Sarah struggled not to be overwhelmed by the oppressive wealth that was displayed with such grandeur—not an easy task when each step brought her past prominently displayed Rubens and at least one Gainsborough. There were gilt

side chairs and a French oval parquetry table with
Derby porcelain figures, even a gilt and bronze
candelabra.

Little wonder Lord Chance possessed such
natural arrogance, she ruefully acknowledged.
Who could not be affected by such surroundings?

Entering the bright green and ivory room,
Sarah discovered Lady Chance on a small sofa.

"My dearest, I thought you would never
come," she cried.

Sarah shifted uneasily, feeling a fraud. "Lord
Chance said you wished to discuss the charades."

Lady Chance waved an airy hand. "Oh, the
charades are but one of a dozen difficulties." She
gingerly scooted over to make space for Sarah
on the sofa. "Please have a seat, and I shall ring
for tea to sustain us."

With decided reluctance, Sarah forced herself
to move forward and perch upon the cushion.
Lady Chance was so genuinely pleased to see her
that it made the entire situation even more
ghastly.

Her faint pangs of guilt, however, were swiftly
forgotten as Lady Chance launched into the details of her upcoming Christmas party.

There were conundrums to decide upon, carols to choose, the appropriate amount of holly
to hang, and the precise spot for the mistletoe.
She also demanded Sarah write down the proper
recipe for the wassail bowl.

After nearly two hours, Lady Chance sat back,
smiling with satisfaction. "How terribly clever you
are, my dear. My party shall be the greatest success, and it shall all be due to you."

Sarah could not help but smile at the effusive
flattery. Although she had never moved in Society,

she was well aware the success of such gatherings depended far more upon who attended rather than what occurred. "I am certain my efforts shall have very little to do with the success of your party."

"But you are too modest," Lady Chance insisted. "How happy I am Oliver discovered you."

Knowing the older woman would not be nearly so happy should she discover the truth, Sarah gave a vague shrug. It was clearly time to take her leave, but before she could find the words to extricate herself, a deep voice spoke from the doorway.

"No more happy than I am," Lord Chance said in soft tones.

In spite of herself, Sarah discovered her gaze clinging to his elegant male form. Hardly surprising, she was forced to concede. Unlike most gentlemen, he wore the tight blue coat and buff pantaloons to advantage. Rather than revealing his various imperfections, they instead emphasized sleek muscles that moved with fluid grace.

With a sudden realization she was staring, Sarah abruptly lifted her gaze to meet his dark, probing regard. Her heart did its familiar leap, but thankfully Lady Chance provided a welcome distraction.

"Oliver."

Lord Chance performed a slight bow. "Mother. Miss Cresswell."

"I did not expect to see you today."

"I thought you would wish to know I have been to Brighton."

Lady Chance clicked her tongue. "So terribly odd of Ben to visit Brighton at this time of year."

Sarah unconsciously bit her lip as she waited for Lord Chance's response.

"I believe he desired a less hectic pace," he said smoothly.

Lady Chance seemed to accept the lie with swift ease. "Poor dear, he did appear a bit drawn when he last visited." She heaved a sigh. "I do not believe London agrees with him."

A sardonic expression settled on Lord Chance's countenance. "He is always welcome to return to Kent."

Lady Chance could not have looked more surprised if Lord Chance had suggested her youngest son sail to the colonies. "Goodness, what would he do with himself?"

"There are any number of duties I would be delighted to share."

Lady Chance wrinkled her brow. "I do not believe Ben cares for such duties."

Sarah bit her lip again, this time to prevent her hasty words. Had Lady Chance ever considered the notion that Lord Chance might not fully care for the burdens he must shoulder? Or that it was hardly fair that Ben be required to care for nothing beyond his own pleasure?

"It would do him no harm to learn a lesson in responsibility," Lord Chance said in neutral tones.

Lady Chance pressed a hand to her breast, her eyes pleading. "He has endured too much, Oliver. We must be patient."

Sarah thought the earl's masculine features hardened, but he gave a ready nod of his head. "As you wish."

A rather awkward silence descended. Well

aware she was out of place, Sarah rose to her feet.

"I should be returning home."

Lord Chance promptly turned in her direction. "I will drive you."

"There is no need."

"I insist."

Well aware that Lady Chance was regarding her with a curious gaze, Sarah had little choice but to concede to the inevitable. "Thank you." Moving forward, she stiffly placed her hand upon his offered arm.

"You will ensure Ben is well, Oliver?" his mother demanded.

"As always." He glanced down at Sarah's troubled eyes. "Come, Miss Cresswell."

Nine

Rumbling along in his carriage, Chance heaved a rueful sigh.

The morning had dawned with a gray drizzle. Warm in his bed, he had lingered far longer than usual before at last rising and making his way down to his breakfast.

Only when he was leisurely enjoying his slice of ham and lightly boiled egg had he been struck by a horrid thought: Surely Miss Cresswell would not be so foolish as to walk to his mother's. It had taken less than a heartbeat for him to have his answer.

For goodness sakes, the woman frequented brothels and placed her school in a neighborhood not even the Watch would enter. She would think nothing of strolling alone halfway across London.

Burning with frustration, he had called for his carriage, nearly pacing with impatience by the time he was at last on his way.

He would never forgive himself if she became ill because of his thoughtlessness, he told himself, especially since he did not even have the excuse of having forgotten her meeting with his mother.

He seemed unable to forget anything connected with Miss Cresswell.

On how many occasions had she disrupted his concentration—and not just at night, when a gentleman's thoughts might reasonably turn to satin skin and enticing lips?

He had assured himself his preoccupation was merely because she was so firmly out of reach. He was like a child who desired a toy simply because it was being denied him.

Well, perhaps not quite like a child, he ruefully acknowledged as he allowed his gaze to study the maiden seated across from him in the carriage. There was nothing childlike in his reaction to her proximity.

Drawing in a deep breath of the lilac-scented air, Chance studied the pure lines of her features and the unreasonable temptation of her lips. Damn, but she was an intoxicating minx, he was forced to concede. More intoxicating than a maiden had a right to be.

His gaze lifted and, with a tiny start, he realized her wide brow was furrowed in a faint scowl.

"You are frowning," he abruptly ended the silence. "Was my mother so horrid?"

She lifted her head and blinked in surprise. "Of course not. She was very gracious."

His lips twisted with a hint of self-mockery. "Then I suppose I am responsible for such a grim countenance. Truly, I wished only to spare you a miserable walk home."

Expecting a tart reply, Chance was startled when she gave an awkward shrug.

"It is nothing."

Intrigued, Chance leaned forward. "Come, I have shared my troubles with you."

There was a long moment when Chance feared she might refuse to confess. Then, entwining her fingers on her lap, she forced herself to meet his gaze.

"I suppose I find it unfair that you should be expected to care for your family while Ben is encouraged to live as he pleases."

Chance stilled, caught off guard by the low words. It was the first occasion anyone had expressed concern for the responsibilities he shouldered. Certainly neither his mother nor Ben considered the vast amount of work their numerous estates entailed. He was the eldest son, and it was his born duty. Until this moment, he would have briskly dismissed any foolish notion that he desired sympathy for his position. Now, however, he could not deny a flare of warmth at the edge of annoyance in Miss Cresswell's tone.

"It seems to be the lot of the eldest child," he said softly. "Do not say you are not expected to be responsible while your sisters do as they please."

"I . . . perhaps," she was forced to concede.

Chance allowed himself a small grimace. "I will not say, however, that Ben should be encouraged to continue his frivolous existence. I fear the influences of London have sadly altered his character. He is in need of something to capture his attention and keep him occupied."

She gave a slow nod, perhaps thinking of her own siblings. "A difficult task."

"Yes." Chance determinedly changed the subject. "Tell me what you accomplished this morning."

"You cannot be interested."

"Of course I am. Since I will be expected to

participate in the various activities, I feel I should
be properly warned."

He had intended to tease a smile to her pale
face, but instead she abruptly stiffened as if she
had been slapped. "I assure you it is all quite
harmless."

Belatedly realizing she had taken his words as
doubting her respectability, he gave an impatient
frown. "I never thought otherwise."

"Even from the daughter of the Devilish
Dandy?"

Chance felt his familiar distaste at her mention
of her father. Really, harboring that roué of an
uncle was bad enough—if he were indeed her
uncle. There seemed little need to constantly ad-
vertise her connection to a notorious jewel thief.

"Why do you do that?" he demanded.

She regarded him warily. "What?"

"Refer to yourself in such a fashion?"

"It is no less than the truth," she insisted. "Just
as you are the son of Lord Chance."

Hardly the same thing, Chance inwardly acknowledged. "No one would know Miss Cresswell
was in any way related to the Devilish Dandy if
you did not make such an effort to announce
the fact."

A guarded expression descended upon her
countenance. "You believe I should dissemble?"

"It might make your path smoother."

Something that might have been disappointment darkened her eyes. "I cannot pretend my
father's behavior is anything but reprehensible,
but he is my father and I love him," she said
with quiet dignity. "I will not lie."

The very simplicity of her words made Chance
flinch. Good gads, he was not usually so insensi-

tive. To have actually suggested she disown her family and lie to the world . . .

And why?

So he should not be ashamed to claim her as an acquaintance?

He was a perfect cad.

"No," he said softly.

"It is who I am. I will not apologize," she said, as if she felt she must emphasize her point.

"Forgive me, Miss Cresswell," he said ruefully. "My words were thoughtless."

She shrugged. "It must be difficult for you to understand."

Chance could not prevent a sudden laugh at the sheer irony of his situation. He leaned back into the soft leather. "Oh, yes. Unlike you, I have no notion of what it might be to possess a relative willing to pinch a necklace or tiara."

Despite her best efforts, her lips gave a telltale twitch. "It is not at all the same, as you well know."

"It is enough to teach me the difficulties of accepting a loved one regardless of his faults."

She lifted a brow. For the moment, neither were aware of the passing houses or the gray drizzle that dampened the cobblestones. "Quite an admission from the Flawless Earl."

He gave a mock shudder, pleased to note a sparkle had returned to her eyes. "Good gads, do not use that ghastly title."

"You are not proud of your impeccable reputation?"

"It is absurd," he retorted, wondering how the devil she had ever managed to hear of the Flawless Earl. "As you have so admirably pointed out, I have many flaws."

"Yes, indeed."

Chance gave a bark of laughter. "My dear, whatever pride I might have possessed you have effectively shredded beyond repair."

She wrinkled her tiny nose. "Pooh."

"I am not in the habit of being poohed."

"Then perhaps it is time you were," she promptly retorted.

Chance thought of all the maidens who had fawned and pandered to his vanity. Not by look or word did they dare imply he was anything but perfect.

Lud, it was no wonder he found Miss Cresswell's pert honesty so refreshing.

"Perhaps it is," he admitted softly.

Their gazes tangled. For a breathless moment, Chance found his thoughts once again turning to satin skin and enticing lips. Then, as if sensing his mounting desire to reach across the carriage and pull her into his arms, she rushed into speech.

"My . . . uncle has been keeping a close guard on Lord Maxwell."

He smiled wryly, wishing Monsieur Valmere and Lord Maxwell to the devil. "Has he?"

"Unfortunately there have been no suspicious movements."

"So once again we must wait."

She lifted her hands. "I fear so."

Chance was not nearly so disappointed as he should be. "Then that is precisely what we shall do."

Nearly holding her breath, Sarah sat at the side of the room as the tiny girl struggled to read aloud the short lesson. Although Fanny had come to the school nearly a year ago, it had taken Sarah months to coax her even to speak. To see her standing before the class and reading aloud made Sarah's heart swell with pride.

As she at last stumbled to an end, Sarah rushed forward to pull Fanny's slight form into a tight hug. "That was lovely, Fanny."

The tiny face flushed with pleasure. "I practiced just as you sez."

"Just as I said." Sarah gently corrected her with another hug.

Leading her pupil back to her seat, Sarah jumped as the door to the classroom was thrown open and Lucky skidded into the room.

"Miss, I think you had best come."

"What is it?"

A wide grin split his narrow countenance. "This you have to see for yourself."

Without giving Sarah the opportunity to question him further, Lucky turned and darted out of the room. Sarah motioned one of the older boys to take charge of the class, and she followed Lucky at a less hectic pace.

She could not imagine what had put Lucky into such a twitter. As a rule, the boy preferred to pretend he was above such childish enthusiasm. She could only suppose a circus was passing or the nearby gin house had once again caught fire.

Moving to the front door that was standing wide open, she found instead two large carts loaded to near overflowing. "Oh," she muttered in shock. "Oh my."

A tall gentleman in a caped greatcoat abruptly leaped from the front cart, which was filled with coal. Sarah's shock only deepened as she realized it was Lord Chance.

"Good morning, Miss Cresswell." He swept a bow.

"What is this?" she breathed.

Straightening, Lord Chance offered her a teasing smile. "Well, the first wagon contains coal, which is generally used to keep a fire burning. The next contains several books, a handful of desks, coats, boots, scarves . . ."

"I can see what they are," she interrupted, "but . . . why?"

He regarded her with an enigmatic expression. "With Christmas swiftly approaching, I began pondering an appropriate gift for you. I assure you I considered a number of more personal items that would delight a young maiden, but it occurred to me you were not like most ladies and that a pearl necklace or ermine muff would not please you nearly so well as a wagon of coal." He paused as he gazed deep into her wide eyes. "Was I mistaken?"

Thrown into confusion by his extraordinary generosity and the tingle of pleasure that he had truly cared to please her, Sarah discovered herself stammering like a widgeon.

"No . . . oh, but you should not have. I mean . . . I expected nothing . . ."

He smiled gently. "Which is what I admire most about you."

She helplessly gazed back at the burdened wagons. "But this is too much."

"It is a gift," he said in low but firm tones. "Surely your father taught you it is only polite to accept such offerings with a gracious air of gratitude."

Sarah knew she should protest. His gesture was far too extravagant for a proper lady. But the realization of how desperately her children were in need of the supplies swept aside her rigid strictures. Instead, her heart filled with a warm glow. She lifted her head to meet his dark gaze. "Thank you."

He reached up to lightly brush her cheek with his gloved fingers. "I have pleased you?"

"More than I could ever adequately express."

The world seemed to halt as he slowly smiled down at her upturned face. "Good."

For a poignant moment, there were only the two of them, and Sarah thought she could stand there in the warmth of his gaze forever.

But of course, nothing was forever. With a loud whistle of appreciation, Lucky moved to join them.

"Cor . . . you be a good 'un, guv," the boy complimented. "When I first seen them fancy togs, I thought you were a flat for sure."

His lips twitching, Lord Chance gave a mocking bow. "I am relieved I have risen in your valuable estimation, brat."

The urchin gave a saucy grin. "Mayhap you be good enough for the Miss after all."

Sarah gasped as her unruly charge gave her a broad wink and scurried back inside to spread the word of their sudden bounty. A flush of embarrassment stained her cheeks as she reluctantly met Lord Chance's glittering gaze. "I must apologize for Lucky. He occasionally forgets his lessons in how to behave as a gentleman."

Sarah could only presume the chill in the air made Lord Chance's cheeks red as he gave a vague shrug. "He is an engaging scamp. You have done well with him."

An awkward silence descended. For the first time realizing she had stepped out without so much as a shawl, Sarah gave a sudden shiver. "I should arrange to have the supplies stored lest they be piled in the center of the kitchen."

"I will gather my men," Lord Chance promised.

Returning inside, Sarah set about arranging the load of supplies being hauled in by a number of footmen. In a surprisingly short time, the carts had been unloaded. Slipping into her office, Sarah put a kettle onto her fire. For a moment she battled her nerves. Then, assuring herself she was only doing what was proper, she stepped out of her office and signaled Lord Chance to enter her private domain. He came without hesitation and firmly shut the door behind his large form.

Sarah felt a brief flare of panic as she realized just how close they were forced to be in the confined space of the office, but, turning to pour them both a cup of tea, she sternly dismissed her ridiculous unease. So what if she could smell the clean scent of his soap and feel the heat from his body? She was certainly mature enough to behave as a lady.

Wasn't she?

Firmly taking command of the situation, she handed him one of the cups. "I thought you had earned some tea."

He smiled as he took a sip. "Ah . . . a private bounty."

"It is the strictest secret," she assured him.

"Nothing could pry the truth from my lips," he promised. Then, as he became aware of her unconsciously probing survey, he lifted his brows. "Why do you regard me in such a quizzical fashion?"

Abruptly realizing she had been staring, Sarah was forced to blurt out the first thing that came to her mind. She could hardly confess she was pondering what it was about this gentleman that so disrupted her normal composure. "I was merely thinking you must have far more entertaining pursuits than carrying coal for schoolchildren."

Thankfully, he appeared to accept her words at face value. "If you are speaking of the various soirees and assemblies, then you are wide of the mark, my dear," he drawled.

"You do not enjoy the social whirl?"

He paused as if debating whether to confess the truth. "I far prefer devoting my time to my collection of Grecian relics," he at last confessed.

Sarah did not need to pretend her surprise. "You are a scholar?"

"A very amateur one." His gaze lowered to inspect the remaining tea in his cup. "Would you desire to see my collection?"

The abrupt invitation caught her off guard. Before she could halt her words, she was giving a pleased nod of her head. "I should like that very much."

His dark gaze abruptly rose. "Thank you."

That breathless sensation once again threatened her, when suddenly the office door was pushed open. Lord Chance moved hastily forward as Mrs. Surton entered the cramped room, at last squeezing in beside Sarah to avoid being run down.

Sarah shivered at the imprint of his large body

pressed close to her own, all too conscious of his breath stirring the chestnut curls atop her head. There was no room, however, to place a more proper distance between them. With as much dignity as possible under the circumstances, she regarded the unexpected intruder. "Mrs. Surton."

"There you are, Miss Cresswell."

"My lord, may I introduce Mrs. Surton? Mrs. Surton, Lord Chance."

Expecting the older woman to punish her with a sermon on being alone with a gentleman, she was surprised when Mrs. Surton did nothing more alarming than nod in Lord Chance's direction. "My lord."

Still uneasy at being caught alone with a gentleman, Sarah rushed into an explanation. "Lord Chance has quite generously donated a number of supplies for the school."

"Oh? How kind."

Sarah frowned, convinced the woman must be ill. It was one thing to overlook Lord Chance's presence in her office. It was quite another to miss the perfect opportunity to preen her own charitable efforts before such an envied member of the *ton*.

"Did you wish to speak with me?" she asked in cautious tones.

"No . . . I simply wished to assure myself all was well with the children."

"Quite well, thank you."

Mrs. Surton awkwardly cleared her throat. "Your uncle is not with you today?"

Sarah felt her heart sink. Good heavens. It was little wonder the woman was so distracted. The Devilish Dandy could make the most sensible

woman behave as a cabbage head. "Ah, no. I fear
not."

"I suppose he prefers to spend such a cold day
before the fire."

The image of her father placidly huddled beside a fire made Sarah choke back a chuckle. Far
more likely he was fleecing some poor soul of
an inheritance.

"I believe he mentioned a visit to the tailor,"
she hastily lied.

"Of course." Mrs. Surton gave a heartfelt sigh.
"Such an elegant gentleman."

"Ah . . . yes."

Abruptly realizing she had revealed more than
she intended, Mrs. Surton straightened in a brisk
motion. "Well, I must not linger. When you do
see your uncle, please give him my regards."

"Certainly."

Nodding, the woman disappeared from the
room. Quite unexpectedly, Lord Chance tilted
back his head to laugh with unabashed amusement.

"Good gads, the most dangerous enemy known
to man . . . a marriage-minded female. I suggest
Uncle Pierre consider a swift return to Paris."

Sarah favored him with a jaundiced glance. "I
could not possibly be so fortunate."

Ten

December arrived with a flurry of snow.

Arising early, Chance stood at his window and experienced a tingle of anticipation. He had always loved the first snow. Perhaps it was childish, but there was something exhilarating in the pristine white that transformed the landscape into a fairyland.

Without giving himself time for second thoughts, Chance abruptly donned his clothes and called for his curricle. He wanted to enjoy the fine morning, and he could imagine no better companion than Miss Cresswell.

Taking the reins himself, he swiftly made his way across town and halted before the small house. He never paused as he tossed the reins to his groom and vaulted onto the street.

Oddly, it never occurred to him as he hastened up the steps that it was far too early to reasonably call on a young maiden. He only knew he desired to see Miss Cresswell on this wondrous morning.

He was kept waiting a moment before the door was at last pulled open by a startled Watts. "Good morning, Watts. Is Miss Cresswell in?"

"Oh . . . yes, this way."

Chance allowed himself to be led up the stairs to the small parlor at the back of the house. Upon entering the room, he discovered Miss Cresswell seated upon a sofa, reading the morning paper. An unconscious smile touched his lips at the sight of her sturdy woolen gown and the manner her curls had been tamed into a tidy bun. She made no effort to attract attention to herself, and yet her natural grace and elegance was far more appealing than any expensive artifice.

His gaze lingered on the purity of her profile, thrown into relief by the blazing fire. There was a great deal of character in that profile, he decided, and an inner strength that made her as exasperating as she was admirable.

As if sensing she was no longer alone, Miss Cresswell abruptly turned her head to regard him with a startled expression. "My lord."

Performing an elegant bow, he offered her his most engaging smile. "Forgive me for intruding at such an unreasonable hour."

"Has something occurred?"

"Actually, it is such a lovely day I wished to take you for a drive."

She gave a swift glance toward the window. "But . . . it is snowing."

"Yes, most perfect weather for a turn in the park," he informed her. Then, as her mouth opened to refuse his request, he swiftly continued, "And you needn't fear. It is far too early in the day for others to be about."

She gave a firm shake of her head. "I do not think that it would be a good notion."

"Why?"

"I will be expected at the school."

"Surely they can survive one morning without you," he said softly.

"Perhaps, but I still feel it would be best if . . ."

"Please come." He overrode her words, uncertain why it was so vital that she agree to his request. "I promise I will not keep you long."

For a moment, Miss Cresswell wavered between propriety and his persuasive pleadings. At last she gave in to temptation. "Very well. I will collect my coat."

It took a few moments for Miss Cresswell to prepare herself for the unexpected outing, but with a minimum of fuss they were comfortably settled in the curricle, and Chance had his bays swiftly headed toward the park.

For a time they rode in a peaceful silence. Then Chance turned to regard his companion. "There, is this not refreshing?"

"It is most certainly brisk," she retorted, shivering.

He gave a low chuckle. "Do you not enjoy the snow?"

"I have to admit I have never given it much thought."

"When I was but a lad, I used to rush to the window every morning in the hope of discovering snow. It made everything magically different, as if I had been given a new land to explore. Does that sound absurd?"

A sudden smile curved her lips. "Not at all. I can just imagine you as a precocious pirate battling snow drifts."

Chance felt his breath catch in his throat. She was so lovely, her cheeks reddened by the sharp breeze and the snowflakes clinging to her tangle of black lashes. His heart gave an odd twinge as he forced his gaze back to the road. "And what made you run to the window in the morning?" he asked in a deliberately light tone.

"I was usually attempting to ascertain where I was," she answered in dry tones. "As you can imagine, we spent little time in any one location."

Chance's smile fled at her words. Damn the Devilish Dandy. How could he have exposed his daughters to such a dangerous and scandalous existence? It went beyond the pale.

"You deserved better," he said as he efficiently turned into the park.

He felt her shrug. "It could have been worse. My father was kind when he recalled we were about, and I always had my sisters near."

Chance battled his instinctive flare of exasperation at her calm acceptance of her fate. "You are very forgiving."

"No," she denied in a low voice, "I simply realize I cannot change the past. I prefer to concentrate on the future."

With little traffic in the park, Chance risked a glance at those amazing blue eyes. "And what do you see in your future?"

Just for a moment her eyes darkened, as if in pain. Then she gave a sharp shake of her head. "I shall no doubt continue with the school."

"What of a family?" he probed, without understanding precisely why.

She slowly lowered her gaze. "I think we both know that is an impossible dream."

Of course he knew it, he told himself. No gentleman could reasonably tie his name to that of a renowned jewel thief. He held a duty to his family and his position to marry a respectable maiden who could bring only honor to their union.

No matter what the temptation.

"It is a bloody . . . deuced situation," he muttered.

As if startled by his fierce tone, she lifted her head to meet his glittering gaze. "I have my sisters and, of course, my . . . Uncle Pierre. It is enough."

"It should not have to be."

"We must accept what fate has given us." She paused for a long moment. "Do you not have your own fate?"

Chance shied from the question. He did not wish to consider the knowledge that his fate included marriage to a staunchly proper maiden who would perform her duty and fill his nursery with heirs. Until this moment, it had never particularly bothered him. Now the mere thought made his stomach twist with distaste.

"It is too lovely a day to spoil with thoughts of fate," he said firmly. "Tell me instead of your sisters."

She flashed him a puzzled frown. "You cannot possibly be interested."

"I am interested in everything about you," he told her softly.

He thought he glimpsed a darkening in her eyes before she firmly turned to offer him her profile. "As I told you before, Emma is a governess and Rachel is staying with friends."

"But what are they like?"

There was a pause before she lifted one shoulder. "Emma is gentle and kind, but very independent."

"Much like you," he murmured.

She ignored his words. "Unfortunately, she is also very troubled by our father. I have tried to ease her pain, but she retreats from others."

"And what of Rachel?"

"Charming, beautiful, and utterly self-absorbed," she promptly retorted.

Chance gave a sudden laugh. "A perfect match for Ben."

A rueful expression softened her features as she turned to meet his teasing smile. "Heaven forbid."

"Yes, indeed," he said. Then, as he noticed the way she wrapped her arms about herself, he gave a rueful smile. "You are cold."

"Perhaps a bit," she admitted.

Without pause, Chance headed for the gate. Once on the road, he deliberately turned toward the fashionable neighborhood nearby. He had traveled some distance before Miss Cresswell at last realized they were traveling even farther from her home.

"Where are we going?"

"You expressed a wish to view my collection," he said smoothly, not about to admit he was simply loath to have their time together come to an end.

"But I cannot go to your home," she protested, shocked.

He sent her a speaking glance. "You visit brothels, but you cannot visit my home?"

"I was concerned with your reputation, not mine," she informed him pertly.

"Being seen in the company of a beautiful maiden can do nothing but enhance my reputation," he drawled.

"Not if they think I am a tart."

He slowly allowed his gaze to sweep her lovely countenance. "No one could ever mistake you for anything but a lady."

She gave an exasperated laugh. "Do you always have your own way?"

Chance pulled his bays to a halt with less than his usual skill. "No," he admitted in low tones. Then, as his groom hurried to take command of the bays, he vaulted to the street and rounded the carriage to help Miss Cresswell alight. Holding her arm in deference to the icy steps, he led her through the front door and into the spacious foyer. He flashed the stunned butler a warning glance as he helped remove Miss Cresswell's cape. "Pate, please have tea sent to the library."

Taking her cape and Chance's coat and hat, the servant gave a jerky bow. "Very good, sir."

Reclaiming Miss Cresswell's arm, Chance firmly steered her toward his private sanctuary. He had no doubt his peculiar behavior would scandalize his staff. Certainly he had never brought any female to his home except his mother. But at the moment he was indifferent to the speculation that might be brewing below stairs. He had awakened that morning with the intention of enjoying his day, and that was precisely what he intended to do.

Sternly thrusting aside the tiny voice that whispered he was behaving in a manner at distinct odds with his reputation as the Flawless Earl, Chance pushed open the door to his library. Intending to lead his guest to the adjoining chamber, he halted as she gave a sudden gasp.

"Good heavens," Miss Cresswell breathed, her gaze wandering over the towering shelves that held hundreds of leather-bound books. "How wonderful."

Chance smiled at her bemused expression. "Do you enjoy books?"

"Very much. I envy your collection."

"I suppose, like most women, you are in alt over Lord Byron?"

"Actually, I prefer Shakespeare."

"Ah, a lady of classical taste," he murmured, his hand raising to gently brush the clinging snow from the curls framing her face. Of their own volition, his fingers moved to trail over her cheek and across the satin softness of her lips.

He heard her sharp breath before she took a step backward.

"You were going to show me your collection."

He dropped his hand and smiled in a rueful fashion. Both knew he had momentarily forgotten his reason for inviting her to his home.

"This way." He walked toward the door across the room and pushed it open, then stepped aside to allow Miss Cresswell to enter before him, remaining beside the door as she directly moved to study the numerous relics housed in glass cases.

In silence she moved from case to case, lingering for long moments to study the etchings he had framed above the cases. The drawings were his own creations of scenes from ancient Greek society that included the artifacts as they might have been used in daily life.

For nearly half an hour, she moved through the room. Chance discovered himself carefully observing her reaction to his beloved treasures. This was the first time he had shared his collection with anyone, though many knew of its existence, and he felt oddly vulnerable. For some reason, it was important that Miss Cresswell not dismiss his fascination as a peculiar fancy.

He was not disappointed.

Slowly turning, she regarded him with a smile of wonderment. "Did you draw these?" she asked softly.

He gave a slow nod. "Yes."

"They are exquisite."

Chance felt a flare of warmth at her obvious appreciation. He could think of no other person whose opinion he valued more. "They are clumsy at best, I fear," he replied as he stepped forward.

She gave a sudden laugh. "Modesty from the Flawless Earl?"

Smiling into her sparkling eyes, he led her to a smaller case in one corner. "I have the jewelry here."

With great care, he pointed out the delicate beads and finely scrolled bits of gold. He was surprised by her swift grasp of his explanations and her probing questions. As a rule, only fellow scholars actually encouraged his vast knowledge of the era. He was even further surprised when she lifted her head to regard him with a determined expression.

"You should have a showing."

"Like Elgin?" he asked, recalling the nobleman's recent display of his marbles.

"Why not?"

Chance pleated his dark brows. "It never occurred to me anyone else would be interested."

"It is a marvelous collection," she assured him. "It should be shared."

"I shall think upon it," he murmured, knowing he had already shared it with the one person who truly mattered. Perhaps someday he would consider a public display, but for now he was satisfied. "Are you ready for tea?"

"Yes."

With a few steps, they were back in the library. After placing Miss Cresswell on a settee near the heavy tea tray, he settled himself close beside her. "Will you pour?"

"If you wish."

With her usual graceful style, Miss Cresswell poured them both a cup of tea and arranged two plates with the numerous pastries. Accepting his plate, he promptly set it aside and turned back to closely study her delicate features.

As if unnerved by his steady regard, she hastily sipped her tea. "I do hope your mother is well," she burst out.

"Well and driving her staff to Bedlam as she prepares for her glorious party."

"And your brother?"

"I have heard nothing, but I predict he shall be back in London within the week."

She gave a faint frown. "I do hope so. We are running out of time."

"Yes," he agreed softly. "I fear you are right."

She set aside her tea and absently reached for a tiny cake to nibble upon. "What will you do if the diamonds are not discovered?"

He shrugged, a sharp tingle of awareness heating his blood as her tongue darted out to capture a stray crumb from her lip.

"Tell my mother the truth and hand the matter over to the runners."

"There must be something we can do," she muttered in frustration.

Chance slowly leaned forward, all thoughts of

the Chance diamonds far from his mind. "Yes, we can enjoy these cakes my chef takes such pride in."

She tensed as she realized how close he had drawn. "They are delicious," she stammered, swallowing her last bite in a rush.

Chance's gaze narrowed at another crumb that lay tantalizingly on her lip. When he had invited Miss Cresswell to join him, he had fully planned to behave as a gentleman. Certainly he would never lure a maiden to his home with the hope of seducing her. Only the worse sort of debaucher would behave in such a shabby fashion. But for all his noble intentions, he discovered Miss Cresswell's unwitting appeal was far more potent than any mere man could hope to resist.

With exquisite care, he stroked his finger over her bottom lip, brushing the crumb away. "There," he breathed in a raw tone.

Her breath rasped through her parted lips. "My lord."

His finger slowly outlined her trembling lips. "I very much wish to kiss you, Miss Cresswell."

She shivered, her eyes wide. "You mustn't."

"No, I suppose not," he agreed with regret. "You could, of course, kiss me."

"Lord Chance."

"Or we could both simply lean forward and our lips would naturally meet."

"My lord," she protested, but Chance did not miss the unconscious manner in which she swayed toward him.

"Just a kiss," he groaned as he wrapped his arms about her and lowered his head. Their lips met, and Chance felt his heart skid to a halt. How soft and willing her mouth was beneath his own.

As soft as a rose petal. He savored the tenderness, gently parting her lips. Until this moment, a kiss had been only a prelude to more enticing activities. Certainly he had never felt his entire body flood with such pure pleasure. Now he thought he would give his entire fortune to hold on to this precise moment.

But, of course, that was impossible. Even as his hands rose to cup her face, his sadly lacking wits made an untimely resurrection. With a deep sigh of reluctance, Chance forced himself to pull away and regard her bemused expression with a rueful smile. "Ah . . . I promised myself faithfully I would behave as a gentleman. It is not normally such a difficult task."

Her head lowered as a flush stained her cheeks. "Perhaps I should go home."

Chance opened his mouth to protest, then, with a flare of regret, realized the wisdom of her words. As much as he might desire to remain with this maiden in his arms, he had overstepped every boundary of propriety. Indeed, he had trampled the boundaries beyond repair—not that he could actually bring himself to rue the impulsive kiss. It had been far too pleasurable for that. But he sensed Miss Cresswell's maidenly confusion. With a smooth motion he rose to his feet. "Yes."

Keeping her head lowered, Miss Cresswell surged to her feet. Chance was wise enough to keep a discreet distance as they made their way to the foyer and retrieved their outer garments. With the same discretion, they climbed into the curricle and made their way across town. He longed to demand what had brought the deep frown to her countenance. Was she furious with his rash behavior or simply as mystified as himself at the attraction between them? But she refused to even glance in his direction, warning him she was in no humor to share her inner thoughts.

Perhaps for the best, he acknowledged with a wry smile. He had no desire to ruin a perfectly lovely day with a well-deserved tongue lashing.

With that thought in mind, he pulled his pair to a halt and escorted Miss Cresswell to the door. Before she could slip away, however, he grasped her hand and raised it to his lips.

"Thank you for viewing my collection," he said softly.

Just for a moment, her head lifted to meet his watchful gaze. He thought he could detect a glow in her beautiful eyes, but before he could determine the emotions flitting across her pale countenance, she abruptly turned and fled into her foyer.

Chance grimaced as he made his way back to his waiting vehicle.

For a gentleman who once presumed he knew everything there was to know about the fairer sex, he was in a devilish fix. Good gads, he had risked his reputation, a revolt by his servants, and his own self-respect, all to spend the morning with Miss Cresswell.

A wise gentleman would plot a strategic retreat at this point.

Pondering his troubles, Chance had just climbed into his curricle when an elegantly attired dandy with a familiar eye patch minced his way down the street. Lifting an ebony cane in Chance's direction, Pierre Valmere advanced to halt beside the vehicle.

"A moment, my lord."

Chance regarded the peculiar gentleman with a hint of wariness. Uncle Pierre was far too smooth for his liking. Not precisely a dirty dish, he acknowledged, but not a gentleman he would ask to hold his purse. And as for being from France . . . well, Chance would lay his last groat that the man was about as French as himself.

Still, he was currently residing with Miss Cresswell, and Chance could hardly be anything but polite. "Monsieur Valmere."

"I have something of interest for you," he murmured, reaching into his pocket to remove a velvet bag. With a few deft movements, he had pulled the strings apart and allowed a long string of pearls to tumble into his gloved hand.

"Pearls?" Chance questioned, wondering if the man was hoping to secure a loan.

As if sensing his less than complimentary thoughts, Pierre flashed him a wicked smile. "Not just pearls. The Maxwell pearls, to be precise," he explained. "Recently sold to an acquaintance of mine for a tidy sum."

"Lord Maxwell," Chance breathed in sudden comprehension.

"I believe so."

"Pearls, not diamonds."

"Yes."

Chance shook his head. He freely admitted he had wanted Lord Maxwell to be responsible for the theft. He not only disliked the scoundrel, but he knew a gentleman would be as anxious as himself to avoid any hint of scandal. Now he was forced to concede his vague hopes were for naught. Maxwell would never have parted with this family heirloom if he possessed the diamonds.

"It appears Lord Maxwell was not involved in the theft," he grudgingly conceded.

"Not unless he is clever enough to sense a trap." Pierre smoothly returned the pearls to his pocket. "A most unlikely notion."

Realizing he owed this gentleman a great deal, Chance performed a half bow. "It appears I am once again in your debt."

The gentleman shrugged as he regarded Chance in a thoughtful manner.

"You were with my niece, *non?*"

Caught off guard by his abrupt question, Chance gave a slow nod. "Yes."

"You will not forget she is a lady?" he murmured, deliberately stroking his hands along the smooth wood of his cane.

Chance did not miss the significance of the gesture. He had no doubt the cane disguised a sword. He possessed a similar one himself. A rather wry smile touched his mouth. He never supposed he would be in the ignoble position of being threatened by a young maiden's guardian.

"I do not forget for a moment," he said in cold tones.

Pierre leaned forward. "I may be old and possess only one eye, but still I see," he warned with a glance that assured Chance he did see—all too well. "Have a care with Miss Cresswell."

Uncertain whether to be embarrassed or furious, Chance abruptly urged his restless horses into motion.

Good gads.

A devilish fix, indeed.

Eleven

The snow had halted shortly after midnight—at half past midnight, to be precise. Sarah was well aware of the time, since she had devoted the greater part of the night staring out her window.

A ridiculous waste of time, she had assured herself, but that did not make sleep any easier to court.

In exasperation, she had at last arisen and attired herself in a sturdy gown. What she needed was something to occupy her mind, she told herself firmly. Perhaps then she would not be so henwitted as to spend the entire night bemoaning her latest foolishness in the arms of Lord Chance.

After all, there was no reasonable explanation for why she found her breath elusive when Lord Chance was near, or why her heart halted when he touched her. Or why his kisses made her burn with an aching need.

It was as incomprehensible as the stars and the moon, and just as hopeless to attempt to alter.

Just a few more weeks, she had assured herself. Just a few more weeks and her time with Lord Chance would be at an end.

On the point of leaving her room and heading

to the school, Sarah was halted as a note was delivered to her door informing her Emma had already called and awaited her in the front parlor.

With hurried steps, she had made her way to the parlor to greet her sister, giving her a hug before pulling her onto one of the tiny sofas.

"What a lovely surprise," she said, smiling.

"I hope this isn't an inconvenient time."

"Don't be a goose. Whenever is it inconvenient to see my own sister?" Sarah teasingly chided.

Surprisingly, Emma did not return her smile. "I wished to catch you before you left for your school."

With an effort, Sarah thrust aside her own troubles to concentrate upon Emma. She was well aware her sister would not have called unless there was something upon her mind.

Pouring them both a reviving cup of tea, she settled herself beside her sister and studied the pale countenance and the unmistakable shadows beneath Emma's eyes.

"You look weary," she said, frowning in concern.

Emma conjured a faint smile. "I must admit the Farwells are rather demanding."

"They are loathsome creatures who treat you more as a slave than a governess," Sarah retorted in blunt tones. Although Emma never complained, Sarah had occasionally called upon her sister, and it had taken little effort to discover the Farwells offered their servants barely concealed contempt and a thorough lack of compassion for their situation. It had taken every effort not to forcibly remove Emma from their poisonous clutches. "I wish you would return to your rooms here."

Emma gave a firm shake of her head. "I cannot. Besides, I have written to Lady Hartshore in Kent. She is seeking a companion."

Sarah felt her heart sink at her sister's words. Although she desperately wanted Emma away from the Farwells, it had never occurred to her she might travel so far away.

"You intend to leave London?"

"If Lady Hartshore will have me."

"But we shall hardly see you," Sarah protested.

An expression of discomfort flitted over Emma's delicate features. "I have decided I should quite enjoy life in the country. Unlike you and Rachel, I have never felt comfortable in town."

Sarah's heart clenched in sympathy. She was well aware Emma's discomfort was not due to London but the scandal of their father. She was also aware her sister hoped by fleeing to the country she could somehow hide from her past. A futile wish, Sarah realized, but she was wise enough to concede that Emma must come to acceptance in her own manner.

"I shall miss you," she said softly.

"Yes, I know." Emma reached out to pat Sarah's hand and smiled sadly. "Of course, it might be that Lady Hartshore shall decide I am not suitable."

Sarah was instantly on her mettle. Emma was the finest, dearest person she had ever met, and she would defy anyone to say otherwise.

"Nonsense. Only the veriest widgeon would not desire you as a companion."

Emma's smile twisted. She was clearly not as confident. "We shall see."

Sarah tilted her head to one side. She sensed that there was more troubling her sister than her upcoming interview with Lady Hartshore. "Is there a reason you wished to speak with me, Emma?"

Surprisingly, a flush of color stained Emma's face as she awkwardly set aside her cup. Sarah felt a twinge of unease as she waited for her sister's confession.

"Yes . . . I . . ." Emma twisted her hands in her lap. "Actually, there has been some talk."

Sarah's unease deepened. Good heavens, did someone suspect that the Devilish Dandy had returned to London? "About Father?" she demanded in anxious tones.

"No." Emma swallowed heavily before lifting her head to meet Sarah's gaze. "About you."

Sarah gave a startled blink. Then, before she could help herself, she was chuckling in disbelief. "Goodness gracious, the rattles must be desperate to turn to me for their source of gossip. What have you heard?"

"Just that Lord Chance has been often seen in the company of a beautiful maiden with chestnut curls and blue eyes. It is also said the lady wears a sapphire pendant."

Sarah shook her head. She might have known any interest in her movements could be directly laid upon the shoulders of Lord Chance. Until he came into her life, the *ton* was thoroughly and thankfully unaware of her presence in London. "And you suspect me?"

Far less amused by the current gossip than Sarah, Emma thinned her lips. "Is it?"

"I am currently attempting to help Lord Chance with a family difficulty," she confessed.

"It is being whispered you are his current mistress."

Sarah stiffened at the blunt words. Although she was frankly indifferent to the rattle mongers, she did care that her sister could think so little of her morals.

"And you've come to inquire if the rumors are true?" she demanded in low tones.

Emma's eyes widened with shock at the question. "Certainly not. I would as soon believe that cows could waltz."

Sarah's heart warmed at the fierce tone. "Thank you, Emma."

"I was merely concerned," Emma said. "As of yet, no one seems to know who you are, but it is only a matter of time."

Sarah shrugged. "I suppose it was bound to occur. Lord Chance is too prominent among the *ton* not to be a constant source of interest to others."

Emma abruptly leaned forward, her expression somber. "You must not see him anymore."

Although it was a tempting thought, Sarah had already dismissed the notion. "I have promised him my help," she said firmly.

A frown touched Emma's brow. "But surely with the gossip you will reconsider?"

"I have never concerned myself with what others might say."

Emma was far from satisfied with Sarah's glib response. "You cannot wish your name to be bandied about in such a fashion."

Sarah could not halt her wry smile. She desperately wished her only concern was what others were saying. It would be far easier to dismiss than the realization Lord Chance was swiftly becoming a vital part of her existence.

"No," she admitted slowly, "but then I cannot

halt vicious tongues from wagging, and I certainly will not allow my life to be ruled out of fear that my actions might raise a brow or two."

Emma sat back in an abrupt motion. "You are not the only one affected," she informed her sister in stiff tones.

Sarah heaved a small sigh. She would never wittingly hurt her sister. Emma had endured enough. But while she could sympathize with Emma's fear of scandal, she could not change who she was. "I am sorry, Emma, but I must follow my heart," she said in firm tones. "I cannot turn my back on those in need, whether it is a child or Madame Vallenway or Lord Chance. It is who I am."

A stricken expression suddenly descended upon Emma's countenance at the low words, and she reached out to grasp Sarah's hand. "Forgive me, Sarah," she pleaded in a husky voice.

Sarah smiled as she patted Emma's hand. "There is nothing to forgive. I am not indifferent to the discomfort you must endure."

"I had no right to come here and criticize," Emma admitted, her gaze filled with regret. "You are such a very good person."

"Poppycock," Sarah instantly denied. "I am opinionated, bossy, and often act without thinking."

"You are the kindest person I know," Emma loyally argued. Then, after a brief pause, she regarded Sarah with a hint of curiosity. "What of Lord Chance?"

Sarah found herself caught off guard. "What do you mean?"

"What is he like?"

"Opinionated and bossy," Sarah promptly retorted.

"As opinionated and bossy as you?" Emma demanded with a faint smile.

"Even more so."

"He is very handsome."

Sarah grimaced. Yes, he was handsome. And intelligent and charming enough to steal the heart of the most elusive maiden. But it was his unexpected kindness she found most unnerving.

How could she remain impervious to his thoughtful gifts for the school? Or his vulnerable delight in sharing his collection with her?

And as for his kisses . . . well, she tried her best not to even think of his kisses.

Why could he not have been a hardened rake or a misogynist, she thought ruefully, or even a pompous fool like most gentlemen she encountered? It would have made her life far simpler.

Of course, a tiny voice whispered, deep down she was not certain she entirely regretted meeting Lord Chance. Her life might have been simpler, but it would have been far duller as well. "Yes, he is very handsome," she at last conceded.

Easily sensing her sister's reluctance to discuss the nobleman, Emma narrowed her gaze. "Do you not like him?"

Sarah paused before she met her sister's gaze. "Sometimes too much."

Emma gasped at the unexpected confession. "Oh, Sarah."

"Do not fear." Sarah briskly sat straighter, her expression determined. "I am a very sensible young maiden and I never forget he is a gentleman quite beyond my touch."

"Do you think it is wise to continue to see him?"

"It is only until Christmas," Sarah said, as much to reassure herself as her sister. "After that I shall never see Lord Chance again."

Never again . . .

Her heart twisted.

With a sense of relief, Sarah heard the gong sound for lunch. With a loud cheer, the children rushed from the room to take their places in the kitchen. Alone, Sarah ruefully regarded the large room scattered with holly, evergreen branches, and decorations the children had painted.

When she had awakened that morning, the day had appeared so gray and dismal she had been determined to find some means of entertaining the children. Preparing for the holiday season had seemed a perfect means of lifting their spirits, and she had to admit it had been an unqualified success. Still, it was nice to enjoy a bit of peace before finishing the greenery that was to be hung on the walls and draped on the fireplace.

Absently gathering the branches that had been discarded, Sarah had just placed them in the bin when the sound of the door opening had her turning about.

Her breath caught at the sight of Lord Chance. It had been nearly a week since she had last seen him, and her gaze eagerly lingered on the deep jade coat that was fitted to his firm body and the glossy Hessians topped by buff breeches. For days she had dreaded his arrival. She had been certain she would feel awkward and embarrassed after their last encounter. But now that he was actually standing before her, she felt nothing but a warm flood of pleasure.

She remained silent as his own gaze roamed over her woolen gown and untidy curls. A brief regret that she was not elegantly attired was banished as a slow smile curved his lips. "Miss Cresswell," he said with a slight bow.

"My lord."

"How very festive the school appears," he complimented as he strolled to stand close beside her.

She wrinkled her tiny nose. "It is far too early to hang the holly, but the days have been so gray that I hoped to lift the children's spirits."

He glanced over the pile of decorations. "I applaud your efforts."

She gave a teasing curtsy. "Thank you, sir."

His dark gaze stroked over her upturned countenance. "You have a gift for making life better for others," he said in soft tones. "A rare gift."

Her heart faltered at his compliment. It was perhaps the nicest thing anyone had ever said to her.

"Was there something you needed?" she demanded in an effort to distract him.

He took a long moment before a rueful smile twisted his lips. "I am uncertain."

Sarah gave a startled blink. Lord Chance uncertain? She would have thought the sky would fall before this utterly confident gentleman would admit to being uncertain of anything.

"I beg your pardon?"

He crossed his arms over the width of his chest. "I awoke this morning with every intention of examining my latest crate from Greece, followed by lunch with Lord Grayson and an afternoon reviewing the accounts from my estate. This evening I had planned to attend two soirees and a ball."

Sarah discovered herself decidedly puzzled by his smooth retort. "It appears you are quite in demand."

"And yet I awoke this morning, dressed, and without even bothering with breakfast, I called for my carriage to drive me here."

Sarah discovered her breath eluding her as she met his dark gaze. "Why?"

He stepped even closer, his hand reaching up to tease the curls about her forehead. "That is what I am attempting to determine."

She knew she should step away, but her legs refused to cooperate. Indeed, it took all her effort not to sway even closer to his large frame.

Thankfully, her shocking weakness was never discovered as a short, heavy-set woman with iron-gray hair bustled into the room. Sarah awkwardly turned as the woman walked directly to the table beside her and placed an armful of greenery on it.

"Here we go, dear."

"Thank you, Mrs. Sparks," Sarah murmured, about to suggest to Lord Chance that he return to his previous plans when he slowly reached out to pluck a tiny bit of greenery with white berries.

"Well, well. What have we here?" he drawled.

"Mistletoe, my lord," Mrs. Sparks promptly retorted.

A devilish grin touched his handsome features. "A most intriguing plant, do you not agree, Miss Cresswell?"

There was a flutter in her lower stomach, but

she managed to shrug. "No more intriguing than any other plant, my lord."

He gave a teasing click of his tongue. "Come now. What of you, Mrs. Sparks?"

Surprisingly, the older woman gave a pleased chuckle. "Well sir, I must admit to a mite of fun beneath the mistletoe when I was a lass. Now I fear I am too old for such nonsense."

"One is never too old," Lord Chance denied. Then, with a languid motion, he raised the mistletoe and placed a chaste kiss on the older woman's cheek.

Mrs. Sparks blushed with pleasure, clearly bewitched by the charming gentleman. "Ah, what a rascal you are," she said. Then she flashed a coy glance at the silent Sarah. "I suppose I should return to the kitchen and ensure the young ones haven't emptied my larder."

With a satisfied smile, the woman hurried out of the room, leaving behind a distinctly wary Sarah. She did not trust Lord Chance in this teasing mood. More importantly, she did not trust herself.

Waiting until Mrs. Sparks had firmly shut the door behind her, Lord Chance held out the mistletoe.

"Now, Miss Cresswell, I believe it is your turn," he said, smiling in anticipation.

Sarah took a firm step backward. She had spent far too many sleepless nights because of this gentleman's kisses. She had no need for more. "Certainly not."

He promptly followed to stand close enough for her to smell the sweet warmth of his skin. "It is tradition."

"Why do you not take it to your soirees and

balls?" she suggested in dry tones. "No doubt there will be a clutch of hen-witted maidens anxious to oblige you."

"No doubt," he readily agreed. "However, I have no interest in hen-witted maidens."

"Perhaps you should, sir."

"Now you sound like my mother," he complained with a grimace. "How she can possibly expect me to reveal an interest in chits who never open their lips except to giggle defies comprehension."

Sarah felt a stab of distaste at his casual reference to the numerous debutantes that filled London. Absurd, of course. She had never desired to gad about Society, and certainly she possessed no wish to be bartered off to the highest title. But somehow the knowledge that this man would soon be choosing his countess from among such maidens left a sour taste in her mouth.

"They cannot be so bad," she forced herself to retort.

"No." He gave a slow shake of his head. "The drawing rooms, of course, are filled with intelligent, well-read young ladies, but for all their numerous charms, not one has lingered in my thoughts."

She wished he would not gaze at her in that manner, she thought as her heart gave a leap. As if there was no one else in the world but her.

"One is bound to, eventually."

"How is that possible when my thoughts are filled by you?" he asked softly.

A poignant warmth flooded her body at his words, but Sarah battled to maintain her composure. "Very charming, my lord."

His brows knit together at her determinedly light tone. "You believe I am flirting with you?"

"Are you not?"

There was a long pause before he at last heaved a sigh. "I wish I knew."

Sarah was not comforted to discover he was as baffled as she by the tug of attraction between them. What did it matter that he desired her as a woman? This time together would soon come to an end, and he would return to his proper debutantes.

"I should be returning to my work," she stiffly retorted.

His hand reached out to gently cup her chin. "Do I not get my kiss?"

Sarah shivered. "I do not think it is wise."

"Sarah." His expression softened, his voice husky with need. "For once can we *not* be wise?"

No, a voice firmly warned her from the corner of her mind, but it was no match for the bittersweet ache that clutched at her heart.

"I . . . yes . . ."

With exquisite care, his dark head lowered. She braced herself for the branding heat of his kiss, but instead his caress was feather light, barely brushing her lips. She shuddered, swaying to lean against his chest. His mouth moved to press against her closed eyes, her wide brow, and down her cheek to the curve of her neck.

"You have bewitched me," he murmured against her satin skin.

Sarah sucked in a shaky breath, inhaling the scent of his soap and the pungent odor of evergreens. She felt intoxicated, as giddy as the first occasion, she had secretly sampled her father's brandy. And just as on that occasion, she knew deep down she was bound to regret her impulsive behavior.

"Please . . ." she at last managed to croak. "You must go."

She felt him still before he was reluctantly pulling away to regard her with a somber expression.

"I will go, but we both know I shall return. I cannot help myself." His head swooped down for one last, lingering kiss. "Good-bye, my dear."

Twelve

When Lord Chance arose the next morning, he was wise enough to resist the urge to seek out Miss Cresswell. He had been absurd to think that a week away from the enticing minx would put an end to his simmering desire. Of course, in his own defense, he had never before encountered a female who had captured his attention past the initial thrill of attraction.

There had been the beautiful countess who had warmed his bed last year, the actress who had caught his fancy during the summer, and the delectable widow who had shared her favors throughout the pleasant autumn. None had managed to stir his interest once he had placed them out of his thoughts for a day or two.

But it had taken only a moment in the company of Miss Cresswell to convince him of his error. Nothing had altered in the long week he had forced himself to avoid her company. She was just as fascinating and just as damnably desirable as ever. And he was just as anxious to pull her into his arms and drown in her sweetness.

It was a wretched mess, he told himself.

Even had he wished to pursue his interest in

Miss Cresswell, it was utterly impossible. She was neither respectable enough to become Countess of Chance nor disreputable enough to become his mistress. And so he was left to battle a desire that could not be satisfied, as well as the guilt of realizing he had done precious little to retrieve the missing diamonds.

Knowing he was far too restless to devote his attention to his studies, Chance called for his carriage and made his way the short distance to his mother's town house.

He was relieved to discover her at home. In short order, he was escorted to the private parlor at the back of the vast house.

Not surprisingly, Lady Chance regarded his entrance with a hint of curiosity. He rarely intruded without notice of his impending arrival.

"Good morning, Mother," he murmured as he crossed to kiss her offered cheek.

"Oliver, what a delightful surprise," she smiled, patting the cushion of the settee. "Shall I order tea?"

He shook his head as he settled his long frame on the cushion, careful not to wrinkle the unfashionably full skirt of his mother's figured silk gown.

"No, thank you."

"Have you heard from Ben?" she demanded in an anxious tone.

Chance was relieved that he had received a message from his brother only that morning. His mother always fretted when her youngest son was not beneath her watchful eye. Not that her watchful eye ever managed to keep his scapegrace brother from plunging into disaster, he wryly acknowledged. But if it brought Lady Chance comfort, that was all that mattered.

"Yes, he should return to London by the end of the week."

Lady Chance clapped her hands in pleasure. "Oh, then he shall be here for my gathering!"

"Who would dare miss the social event of the holiday season?" he drawled, a glint in his eyes.

"Hardly that, but it should be quite diverting." His mother preened. Then she gave a faint frown. "Of course I do wish you could convince Miss Cresswell to attend. Such a charming girl."

Chance stiffened. He had come to his mother's to put Miss Cresswell out of his thoughts. The last thing he desired was to discuss her numerous charms. "She appears quite adamant," he said in dismissive tones.

The older woman gave a faint pout. "I do not believe you have even attempted to convince her."

He lifted his dark brows at the accusation. "What would make you presume such a thing?"

"Well, she is obviously in love with you," Lady Chance shocked him by retorting. "Had you asked her to attend, she certainly would."

Chance surged to his feet in an awkward motion. He felt as if he had taken a blow to the stomach. "You are mistaken, Mother. Miss Cresswell is not in love with me," he rasped.

Lady Chance regarded him in vague bewilderment. "Then why was she seen driving in the park with you?"

Blast the London rattles, he silently cursed. Why could they not mind their own affairs? Miss Cresswell was above reproach. Indeed, she lived a life more full and worthy than any of the supposed *ton*. The thought that her name was being bandied about was untenable. "You should not listen to such worthless gossip," he told his mother.

"Then she was not with you?"

"Yes, but . . ." Chance halted in exasperation. Good gads, he could not explain his complex relationship with Miss Cresswell to his mother. He did not comprehend it himself.

A decidedly curious expression descended upon the older woman's countenance. "Why, I have never seen you so flustered, Oliver."

Chance did not miss the hopeful note in his mother's voice, a hope he was swift to dismiss. "Please, Mother, do not suppose that I am considering Miss Cresswell to become the next Lady Chance."

"Why ever not?" the current Lady Chance demanded. "She is beautiful, charming, and not at all intimidated by you."

His lips twisted. "Yes, I know."

"And I am not so old that I did not notice the way your gaze lingered upon her," she continued slyly.

Chance briefly closed his eyes. Of course his gaze had lingered. He truly believed he could gaze upon Miss Cresswell for the remainder of his days.

"It is impossible."

"Why?"

"Because she . . ."

"Oliver, for goodness sakes, what is it?" his mother demanded with a sharp impatience.

Feeling unjustly harassed, Chance realized that he would have to confess the truth. Now that his mother had taken the maggot into her head that Miss Cresswell would be a suitable daughter-in-law, she would drive him to distraction with her matchmaking efforts.

"She is the daughter of the Devilish Dandy," he burst out in blunt tones.

A stunned silence followed his words as Lady Chance struggled to accept the truth. "The jewel thief?"

"Yes."

The color drained from his mother's round face. "Oh . . . and she seemed like such a lady."

Chance had intended to convince his mother of Miss Cresswell's unsuitability as a prospective bride. How else could he have any peace otherwise? But, perversely, her shocked words made his countenance tighten with annoyance.

"She is a lady," he insisted in tones that defied argument. "Whatever her father has done is not a reflection upon her."

Lady Chance clicked her tongue. "Unfortunately, Society would not agree. A maiden is judged not only on her beauty and accomplishments, but also on the purity of her reputation and that of her family. Such a pity."

The stark truth of her words only served to deepen Chance's irritation. "It is dashed absurd," he gritted. "Miss Cresswell is more worthy than of all those supposedly respectable maidens rolled into one."

A gathering frown darkened Lady Chance's brow at his fierce defense of Miss Cresswell. Whatever her hopes for luring her son down the aisle, they had been effectively dashed by the knowledge the young woman was connected to the Devilish Dandy. Now she was clearly concerned that her son was far too staunch a supporter for the scandalous miss.

"Perhaps, but it would not be wise to be seen in her company, my dear," she said with delicate caution. "You do have your own reputation to think of. Thank goodness she possessed the good sense to decline my invitation."

Chance grimaced. "Oh, yes, Miss Cresswell is utterly sensible to her position."

"More sensible than you, I fear."

Chance was unable to prevent the harsh laugh that echoed eerily through the vast room. "I assure you I am ever conscious of it, Mother." He gave a shake of his head. "That does not, however, prevent me from desiring to be with her."

"Oh, Oliver," his mother gasped in dismay.

"Yes, foolish of me, is it not?" he mocked himself. "I have always prided myself on being the most intelligent of blokes."

A woman who disliked any sort of discord in her life, Lady Chance struggled to make the best of the unexpected troubles. In her mind it was always best to ignore unpleasantness in the hope that it would simply go away.

Drawing in a deep breath, she settled back in the settee. "It is a passing fancy," she proclaimed in determined tones. "After all, she is pretty and possesses quite pleasing manners. You will soon meet another to push all thoughts of Miss Cresswell from your mind."

"So I have told myself," he retorted in dry tones.

"It must be a passing fancy," she repeated with a firm expression.

Chance had no need for his mother's warnings.

He had brooded upon the dilemma far too often not to have come to the same conclusion. "Yes."

"Perhaps you should return to Kent until the Season begins."

Chance shook his head. It was an enticing thought. Surely miles from London and surrounded by the ancient and noble legacy of the Chance dynasty, he could thrust Miss Cresswell from his thoughts once and for all. But he dismissed the notion as swiftly as it entered his head. A few miles and a pile of old stones were not the cure for his troubles.

"I am not one to flee from my problems." He deliberately eased his rigid muscles. "Besides, how could I miss your grand party?"

Lady Chance's expression remained one of concern. "Please do not think that I do not like Miss Cresswell," she pleaded. "She is most charming. It is just . . ."

"Yes, I know," Chance said wearily. "I must go."

Lady Chance slowly rose to her feet. "Take care, Oliver."

Huddled in the corner of the carriage, Sarah attempted to keep her gaze from straying toward the heartbreakingly familiar gentleman across from her. It had been nearly a week since she had last seen Lord Chance, and it was proving amazingly difficult not to simply stare at him in open pleasure.

Who would have thought such a sensible maiden could devote hours to brooding upon the taste of a gentleman's lips, the scent of his skin, and the extraordinary way he gazed into her

eyes? Or pace the floor long into the night battling the disappointment that he did not call
upon her?

It was all as confusing as it was vexing, and
Sarah wavered between tears of self-pity and anger at her foolish weakness.

At least it would all soon come to an end, she
attempted to reassure herself. Lord Chance had
arrived on her doorstep earlier that morning with
the announcement that Ben had returned to London. Gathering her courage, she had demanded
to be taken to him at once. At last she would have
the opportunity to assure herself she had done all
that was possible to locate the Chance diamonds.
After that, she would be in the position to wash
her hands of Lord Chance once and for all.

Which was precisely what she desired, was it
not?

Absently plucking at the skirt of her russet
gown, she heard the whisper of leather as Lord
Chance leaned forward. "You are very quiet." He
broke the long silence.

With a great deal of reluctance, she lifted her
head to meet his searching gaze. "I am concerned." She attempted to divert him from her
true troubles.

"About meeting Ben?" he questioned in genuine surprise. "I assure you he is remarkably harmless. Indeed, you will find him far more pleasing
than myself."

Impossible, Sarah silently acknowledged even as
she shook her head.

"I am concerned I am wasting all of our time.
After all, Ben might not be able to shed any sense
on the bumble broth."

"We shall not know until we try."

"Yes, I suppose you are right," she agreed, sighing.

His dark gaze narrowed as it studied the paleness of her countenance and the shadows beneath her blue eyes. Since arriving that morning, Lord Chance had maintained a polite but distant manner. Not by look or deed had he attempted to take advantage of the humiliating weakness she had revealed during their last encounter. In truth, Sarah suspected he was determined to squash any hopes she might harbor of further intimacies, a thought that made her cringe in embarrassment.

His expression, however, at the moment was softened with concern. "Are you certain there is nothing else troubling you?"

For a mad moment she wondered how he would react if she confessed the truth—that she was troubled by the way her body ached for his touch, by the way she felt only half alive when he was not near, and how she awoke in the midst of the night terrified she might never see him again.

Of course, she did nothing so foolish. Instead, she forced a stiff smile to her lips. "What could be troubling me?"

"I should very much like to know," he said softly.

She breathed out in relief as the carriage rolled to a halt. "We have arrived."

He paused, as if considering whether or not to pursue his question. Then, with a barely audible sigh, he smoothly climbed out of the carriage and helped her alight.

The earlier snow had given way to a dismal rain, and they hurried up the short path to the modest house. Within moments, a butler had ushered them into the foyer and relieved them of their outer wraps. From there they were led to a small parlor, where a slender, boyishly handsome gentleman was absently pacing the floor.

At first glance there was little resemblance between the two brothers. Ben was built along delicate lines, with lighter hair and features that held none of the forceful character of Lord Chance. Not until he smiled did Sarah feel the tangible charm that was so evident in his older brother.

"You are looking well, Chance," the younger man said, his gaze lingering on the perfectly knotted cravat and fitted emerald coat.

"As are you, Ben." Chance firmly drew Sarah forward. "May I introduce Miss Cresswell? Miss Cresswell, my brother, Mr. Coltran."

Ben performed a credible bow. "Your servant, Miss Cresswell."

"Mr. Coltran."

"Chance has told me of your efforts. I cannot express my gratitude."

"I fear I have been remarkably unsuccessful thus far," she felt compelled to confess with a small pang. She could easily understand Lord Chance's urge to protect his younger brother from his own foolishness. There was something very weak and vulnerable in his delicate features. "That is why I wished to speak with you."

Ben grimaced as he moved to pour himself a large measure of whiskey.

"I do not know how I can be of help. I haven't the foggiest notion what happened to those bloody . . . er . . . deuced diamonds."

Sarah wisely overlooked his less than delicate language. The poor boy was clearly overwrought with a combination of guilt and fear, and, like most weak men, he lived in dread of having his misdeeds revealed.

"Perhaps you know more than you realize," she encouraged.

"What do you mean?"

"I wish you to tell me every detail of the evening that you took the diamonds."

Ben shoved an impatient hand through his brown curls. "I already told Chance . . ."

"Ben," Lord Chance abruptly interrupted in stern tones. "Do as Miss Cresswell requests."

Instantly cowed by his more forceful brother, Ben gave a rather petulant shrug.

"Very well. As I told Chance, I went to Mother's with Goldie and borrowed the diamonds. Then we came back here."

Sarah, determined, drew a mental image of that evening in her head. "When you returned, did you go straight to the safe?"

Ben wrinkled his brow. "Yes."

"Where is it kept?"

"Over there." He waved his hand toward a rather horrid landscape framed on the wall.

Crossing the room, Sarah discovered the latch on the frame with a skill learned from her father and allowed the painting to swing open. Cut into the wall, the safe was not particularly sophisticated and no doubt could have been broken into by an experienced thief within a blink of an eye. After studying the lock with an experienced gaze, she at last turned back toward Ben. "So you opened the safe and put the diamonds inside."

"Yes . . ." Ben faltered, his frown deepening. "No, wait."

"What is it?" Lord Chance demanded.

Struggling to recall the precise events, Ben absently set his glass aside. "Masswell came to the door and announced that Moreland and Fritz had arrived."

Sarah watched him closely. "What did you do with the diamonds?"

"I must have put them in the safe."

"Are you certain?" she coaxed.

There was a long pause as Ben bent his powers to dredge up the memories. Then suddenly he gave a sharp shake of his head.

"No, I remember. I gave the diamonds to Goldie and told him to put them in the safe."

Sarah felt a flare of excitement. At last they were getting somewhere. Still, she was cautious not to allow her vague suspicions to encourage her to leap to conclusions. "Did you leave the room?"

"Yes, I went to get rid of my guests."

Sarah slowly advanced toward the young gentleman. "Think carefully, Mr. Coltran. When you returned, did you see the diamonds in the safe?"

There was another pause as Ben thought back. "No," he at last admitted. "Goldie had already locked them in."

Her suspicion only deepened. "Did you check on them anytime that evening?"

"No."

"So you never saw the diamonds after you requested that Goldie put them in the safe?"

Clearly baffled by her persistence, Ben heaved an exasperated sigh. "No."

Beside him, however, Lord Chance was not nearly so slow-witted. Glancing from Sarah to the safe and back to her, a slow dawning of comprehension swept across his countenance. "Good Lord," he breathed.

Ben turned to his older brother. "What is it?"

Lord Chance's gaze never strayed from Sarah's wide eyes. "Goldie," he said in firm tones.

Sarah smiled with a flare of satisfaction. "Precisely."

Thirteen

Chance regarded Sarah's lovely face with a warm flare of admiration. Good gads, he had known beautiful women and, on rare occasions, truly good women. But none had managed to combine such virtues with an innate intelligence that never failed to amaze him.

She was astonishing.

With a few intuitive questions, she had delved straight to the truth of the events on that fateful evening and determined precisely what must have occurred rather than accepting matters as they seemed to have occurred. Not even he had thought to ensure that the diamonds had actually made it to the safe, or to suspect the most obvious culprit.

Astonishing, indeed, he silently conceded.

Lost in her startling blue eyes, he had nearly forgotten his brother. In truth, at the moment he wished to forget all but her.

Ben, however, was predictably impervious to the silent exchange between Chance and Sarah as he struggled to comprehend what was occurring.

Shaking his head, he glanced toward his older brother. "What about Goldie?"

Chance drew in a deep breath. Although Ben was not the most clever of gentlemen nor the most responsible, he could be blindly loyal to those he called his friends. It was hopeless to assume he would readily accept their suspicions. "He is the one who stole the Chance diamonds."

A gasp of shock rasped through the air. "Ridiculous. Goldie is not a thief," Ben retorted in outraged tones. "Besides, he put the diamonds in the safe."

Chance folded his arms across his chest. "You said yourself you never saw him put the jewels in the safe. It would have been a simple matter to slip them into his pocket, close the safe, and await your return."

A peevish expression descended upon Ben's boyish features at the utterly logical explanation. "Not only is Goldie a gentleman, he is my friend. He would never treat me in such a shabby fashion."

Chance possessed far less faith in the dull-witted dandy. He had already discovered from Ben's acquaintances that Goldie had all but disappeared and that he was clearly in dun territory.

"Can you deny he was pressed for money?" he demanded of his brother.

Ben's lips turned down at the edges. "Gads, who is not besides the Flawless Earl?"

Chance stiffened in anger. Damn the bloody fool. He had gone to great lengths to attempt to save Ben from his latest bout of stupidity. He should be showering him with gratitude, not offering up childish insults. "Both Miss Cresswell and I have come here to help you, Ben, at considerable inconvenience to both of us," he said in soft warning.

The younger gentleman bunched his shoulders in a defensive fashion. "Well, I do not like to have my friend branded as a thief."

"There is no other explanation."

"Anyone could have slipped in and stolen those jewels."

Chance stepped forward, a hint of exasperation in his dark eyes. Really, Lady Chance had done the young gentleman no favors in keeping him forever a spoiled child. The world, with all its disappointments and responsibilities, was bound to catch up with him eventually.

"But no one knew you had them," he said with low insistence. "What thief would have chosen the home of a bachelor who is notoriously without a feather to fly with when only two streets away lives the finest collector of Renaissance painters in all of London?"

Clearly unable to deny the logic in his arguments, Ben tried another path. "Then one of the servants."

Chance gave a relentless shake of his head. "Their rooms have already been thoroughly searched. There are no diamonds."

Ben met his unwavering gaze for a moment. Then, with a frown he turned toward the silent Miss Cresswell. "It isn't possible."

She offered him a sympathetic smile. "I admire your loyalty, Mr. Coltran, but every evidence leads to the same conclusion."

"It is a mistake." Ben ridiculously refused to concede defeat.

Swiftly losing what little patience he still possessed, Chance stepped forward. "Tell me, have you seen Goldie since the night the diamonds disappeared?"

"Well, I . . ." Ben faltered before giving a reluctant shake of his head. "No, no, I haven't."

"Do you not think it odd that he has not called?"

"I have been away."

"He did not call before you left, nor since your return."

The faintest hint of doubt suddenly rippled over Ben's countenance. "That does not mean he stole the jewels."

"Use your wits, Ben." Chance pressed his advantage. "Goldie was in need of money, he possessed the perfect means of stealing the diamonds, and now he has all but disappeared."

Far too stubborn to yield easily, Ben shuffled his feet. "I will not believe it until I see the diamonds in his hands."

Chance opened his mouth to utter a sharp retort but halted as Sarah intruded into the brotherly squabble.

"Then that is what we shall do."

Chance shot her a startled glance. "Do you have a scheme in mind?"

She hesitated as if still considering her plot. "We need to force Goldie to reveal where he has hidden the diamonds."

"If he has them," Ben intruded.

Sarah merely smiled. "Of course."

Chance paced across the carpet, pondering the various means of retrieving the jewels. The mere thought of them in the hands of that witless scoundrel was enough to make his stomach twist with distaste. "I could throttle the truth from him," he suggested.

"Not precisely what I had in mind," Sarah declined his vengeful offer.

Chance halted to regard her with a steady gaze. "Lucky?"

Again she paused, then gave the smallest shake of her head. "I think we shall be more direct." She turned toward the younger gentleman. "Mr. Coltran, I wish you to visit Goldie."

"By gads, I have every intention of visiting him, if only to prove this is all a mare's nest," Ben readily growled.

"Yes, yes." She soothed his wounded sensibilities, but there was a hint of iron in her expression. "But I wish you to tell him you have recovered the Chance diamonds."

Ben blinked in confusion, and on this occasion Chance could not condemn him. He was having his own difficulties maintaining pace with her agile mind.

"Eh?"

Sarah moved to stand directly beside the young gentleman. "Tell him a man approached you and demanded a ransom for the Chance diamonds, which you naturally paid, and that you received the jewels in return."

"But that is absurd," Ben sputtered. "I do not have the diamonds."

Sarah heaved a faint sigh at his slow wits. "Yes, I know, but Goldie will not realize that."

Ben gave a restless shake of his head. "I do not comprehend how such a Banbury story will prove Goldie has the diamonds."

"You must frighten him with the fear you now possess the diamonds," she explained, maintaining her patience with a heroic effort. "That is our only means to force him to reveal where he has them hidden."

Chance stilled as the simple brilliance of her plan at last formed in his mind. Good gads, it was a lucky thing that she had not chosen to follow in her father's footsteps, he wryly acknowledged. London would not have been safe from such cunning. "Of course," he breathed.

Still baffled, Ben glanced toward his older sibling. "What?"

"If you have the diamonds, it can only mean someone has stolen them from him," Chance retorted, a smile of anticipation curving his lips. "Goldie will certainly search to see if he has been robbed."

Sarah flashed him a pleased glance at his ready understanding. "And we shall be watching to discover where he searches."

Resisting the urge to cross the room and pull her into his arms, Chance contented himself with an elegant bow. "Brilliant as ever, Miss Cresswell."

Her expression became rueful. "We have yet to determine if such praise is due."

Planting his hands on his hips, Ben glared at the two of them in exasperation. "Will someone kindly tell me what the devil is going on?"

It was decided that the scheme to entrap Goldie would be attempted on the following morning. Chance bridled at the delay. The diamonds were within his reach, and he did not wish to waste a moment in returning them to their rightful place. Still, he could not deny the sense in Sarah's desire to coach Ben in his part of the

ploy. And, of course, she had insisted Ben reveal
the layout of Goldie's home in exacting detail,
as well as make a list of every servant he could
recall seeing within the household. There was
also the necessity of planning how Chance and
Sarah could slip into the house unnoticed. It was
at last decided that Lucky would use his ingenuity
to clear a path for the entrance. Chance possessed full confidence in the crafty lad's ability.
He was quite as intelligent as his mistress.

Soon after that, Chance escorted Sarah home.
She had been oddly silent, and Chance had discovered himself reluctant to intrude upon her
thoughts. What did they have to say, after all?
They were both aware that if the diamonds were
indeed discovered, their time together was at an
end. After tomorrow, they might never see one
another again.

It was a sobering thought, he had to acknowledge.

And a decidedly painful one as well.

The uncomfortable ache plagued him for the
rest of the day and far into the night. It was only
after he sternly warned himself that Sarah's very
safety depended upon his concentrating on the
task at hand that he managed to shove aside the
dark image of their imminent parting.

First they must find the diamonds. Then he
could consider the future.

Keeping that thought firmly in mind, he col-
lected Sarah and Lucky the next morning before
driving to the mews behind Goldie's home. They
waited in the decidedly crisp air until certain Ben
had arrived at the appointed time. Then, sending
Lucky ahead of them, Chance and Sarah crept
toward a side door that led directly to the library.

It would be the obvious place for a safe. More importantly, they would be just across the hall from the parlor where Goldie received his guests. They should be in position to overhear every word between Goldie and Ben.

Hidden beside the door, Chance did his best to block the cutting wind from the slender maiden. It had occurred to him to command that Sarah remain safely at home. He had no desire to see her placed in such potential danger, but the notion had lasted only a moment. Not only had Sarah committed a good deal of time and energy to recovering the diamonds, she was quite likely to condemn him to the devil for suggesting that she miss the crowning moment. It was not in her to remain cravenly at home, no matter what the danger.

The sudden sound of shouts, followed by pounding footsteps, brought Chance sharply to his senses. It sounded as if the entire household had abruptly decided to bolt down the street at breakneck speed. He glanced downward to discover Sarah stifling a giggle.

"Good gads, I have never heard such a commotion," he whispered.

"Well, we did request that Lucky give us a diversion."

"What did he do?"

"He passed the servant's entrance and called out that a carriage had overturned and a chest of coins had spilled onto the road."

Chance chuckled in appreciation. "Your notion?"

"Uncle Pierre," she corrected.

"Cleverness runs in the family, I see."

She grimaced, looking utterly adorable despite her drab cape and plain bonnet.

"Let us hope it has accomplished its purpose."

"Yes," he breathed, his hand reaching up of its own accord to capture her chin in a gentle grasp. "Sarah?"

Her soft lips parted as she gazed into his dark eyes. "What is it?"

"I know better than to forbid you to be present when Goldie is exposed," he said in soft tones, his expression somber. "But I wish you to remain in the shadows."

Her brows lifted. "You fear for my reputation?"

"No, I fear for you," he rasped. "If Goldie was desperate enough to steal the diamonds there is nothing to say what he will do when threatened with exposure."

"And what of you?" she demanded.

Releasing his grasp, he reached into his greatcoat to reveal a deadly pistol. "I came prepared."

Surprisingly she did not flinch or cry out at the sight of the gun. Indeed, she merely shrugged before reaching beneath her cape to reveal a pistol of her own. "As did I."

His eyes widened before he was choking back a laugh. Damn, but the chit had brass.

"Oh, Sarah." He gave a rueful shake of his head. "Still, I want your promise that you will remain behind me."

She paused before giving a faint shrug. "I will try."

It was the best he would get from the willful maiden, and Chance nodded his head. "It is time."

With silent movements, Chance pushed open the narrow door and slipped into the shabby library. He took a careful glance around before motioning Sarah inside and shutting the door. Together they moved across the room until they could hear voices floating through the hallway.

Taking Sarah's arm, he pulled her between two of the bookcases that lined the walls. The feel of her slender form pressed so intimately next to his own made him briefly close his eyes in bittersweet pleasure. Gads, but it felt so utterly right to have her pressed next to him, her feminine scent filling his senses. So right that it was impossible to think she might never be so near again.

Wrenching open his eyes, he desperately attempted to concentrate on the disembodied voices floating through the air.

"I do not believe I could have heard you correctly." The stunned voice of Goldie. "Did you say you have the diamonds?"

Chance felt Sarah stiffen as she awaited Ben's well-rehearsed response. All depended upon his brother's ability to convince Goldie the jewels were now in his possession.

"Devilish queer thing," Ben slowly retorted. "Man arrived on the threshold with the jewels and demanded a bloody ransom. Paid, of course, though it went against the grain, I must tell you. Can't have the family heirlooms in the hands of a blighter."

"And you are certain they are the Chance diamonds?" Goldie's voice sounded strained.

"Should know my own diamonds."

"Oh, yes . . . quite."

"Still, it is odd," Ben continued, precisely as Sarah had instructed.

"What?"

"Can't see how he got them. Swore a scoundrel had sold them to him. Sounds a bit havey cavey to me."

There was a tension-filled silence. "So you still do not know who stole them?"

"Some blackguard, no doubt."

"Yes." Goldie's murmur was barely audible.

Clearly having tested his ability to dissemble to its fullest, Ben loudly cleared his throat. Chance winced at the clumsy warning of his upcoming departure.

"Well, I'm off to the club. Will you come?"

Chance held his breath. If Goldie were willing to leave then their suspicions would be for naught. No gentleman suddenly afraid that price-less jewels had been stolen from him could blithely toddle off to the club.

Thankfully, his brief moment of unease was swiftly banished.

"No . . . no, I have . . . ah, I must call upon my man of business."

"Pity. Thought we should celebrate," Ben urged.

Chance felt a stab of pity. His brother would be deeply cut by his friend's treachery.

"Tomorrow, perhaps," Goldie hedged.

"Very well."

"Now I fear you must excuse me."

"Devilish hurry, ain't you?" Ben complained.

The voices grew louder as Goldie escorted his friend toward the front foyer. "Shouldn't like to be late. Shall I call on you tomorrow?"

"None too early, mind," Ben warned.

"Certainly not."

Their voices faded out of earshot, and Chance glanced down at the woman beside him. Her countenance was pale but resolute, and he offered her an encouraging smile. What other woman would stand beside him with such courage, he wondered? The temptation to steal a brief kiss was sternly repressed as he forced himself to listen for the returning footsteps. He had to be prepared in case he was forced to follow Goldie to some other part of the town house.

It appeared for the first time in weeks he was in luck. Within moments, Goldie's short, rather plump form appeared within the library and crossed directly to the far wall.

Chance cautiously edged in front of Sarah as the gentleman shoved aside the picture that covered the wall safe. With visibly shaking hands, he at last managed the lock and pulled open the small door. His harsh breath of relief could be heard through the room as he hastily pulled out a sparkling diamond necklace and tiara.

Chance felt a rush of relief at the realization the Chance diamonds had indeed been discovered. Sarah had been right.

Lifting his gun, he moved silently to the center of the room. "Lovely jewels, are they not, Goldie?" he drawled.

With all the drama of Kean, Goldie spun about, a look of horror pasted upon his face. "You . . . how . . ."

"It does not matter how." Chance held out a slender hand. "I will take those."

There was a charged moment as Goldie desperately clutched the vast fortune in his hands. Then, noting the unrelenting expression of the much larger gentleman and the pistol pointed directly at his heart, he gave a wretched shudder.

Inching forward, he dropped the jewels into Chance's hand.

"I never meant to take them," he blubbered, his round face beaded with sweat. "Ben gave them to me to put in the safe. But then . . . I so desperately needed the money and they were there and I . . . I couldn't resist."

Chance felt little sympathy for the terrified young man. He had cravenly stolen precious family heirlooms. Even worse, he had stolen them from his own friend. He was a weak and immoral fool. "Ben trusted you," he charged in low tones.

Goldie ran a hand nervously through his pale curls. "I know. That was why I could not sell them, despite those horrid moneylenders." He licked his dry lips. "What will you do with me?"

Chance's first impulse was to hand him over to the authorities and allow justice to take its due course. It was, after all, what he deserved. But the knowledge his mother was bound to discover the truth of Ben's own betrayal if there were a trial made him hesitate. He had gone to far too much effort to protect his family to toss it away on a selfish desire for vengeance.

"For Ben's sake, I will give you the opportunity to return to your home in York," he said in cold tones, his expression a harsh warning. "Do not return to London, or I will expose you for the thief you are."

Goldie's pudgy hands flew outward. "I did not mean to take them."

Unmoved, Chance narrowed his gaze. "I suggest you begin packing."

Fourteen

With a pang of sympathy, Sarah watched Mr. Coltran angrily pace the floor of his parlor. It was obvious the poor boy was thoroughly distraught at the realization his closest friend had betrayed him in such an infamous manner. It was never easy to have one's trust so abused. But Sarah's sympathy was not solely induced by the young gentleman's disillusionment. Although Ben might be too busy nursing his feelings of outrage to notice his older brother standing to one side, Sarah was vibrantly aware of his every move and expression.

It was obvious to her that now the relief of discovering the diamonds had passed, Lord Chance was giving thought to the part his brother had played in the theft. It was also obvious that his brooding brought him little pleasure.

Sarah sighed at the impending unpleasantness. Ben was far too spoiled to take his punishment with grace. There was bound to be an angry scene.

Abruptly turning on his heel, Been slammed his fist into his open palm. "A bloody bad day when a man cannot trust his own friends," he burst out.

Lord Chance slowly strolled forward, his expression decidedly lacking sympathy. "I shouldn't take it so hard, Ben. Goldie is like most dandies. Frivolous and self-centered, with little constitution for facing unpleasantness. He saw the means of putting an end to his troubles and was simply too weak to resist temptation. For what it is worth, I do believe he regrets his actions."

Ben gave a loud snort of disgust. "He jolly well should. Do you know how many sleepless nights I have spent?"

Lord Chance glanced down his slender nose. "No more than you deserve, I am certain."

Ben reddened, but refused to display any hint of remorse. "I shouldn't need to have any if Goldie hadn't turned scoundrel."

"He was no more a thief than you, Ben," Lord Chance said in cool tones.

Sarah bit her bottom lip as Ben visibly bristled at the accusation. "I did not steal the diamonds. I merely borrowed them."

Lord Chance was patently unimpressed by the fine distinction. "You stole them as surely as Goldie did, and for the same selfish purpose."

There was a tense silence before Ben's gaze abruptly dropped. "Well, it has all sorted itself out," he muttered.

"Thanks only to Miss Cresswell."

Sternly prompted by his brother, Ben obligingly turned to offer the silent Sarah a hasty bow. "Oh, yes. I am ever in your debt, Miss Cresswell."

Sarah gave a rather embarrassed shrug. "I am only happy that the diamonds were found."

Reluctantly turning back to his brother, Ben

shuffled his feet in a nervous fashion. "I suppose I should return the diamonds to Mother."

"Oh, no. I shall return them," Lord Chance announced in firm tones.

A hint of color stained the younger man's countenance. "Will you tell her the truth?"

"No. Only because I do not wish to wound her with your treachery."

Ben's expression became petulant at the chiding words. "You needn't make such heavy weather of the matter."

Lord Chance gave an exasperated click of his tongue. Sarah could readily sympathize with his growing impatience. Ben reminded her strongly of her younger sister Rachel. Both were blessed with beauty and charm that ensured they were readily spoiled by admiration, and both possessed a selfish need to put their own happiness before those of others, just like children who could see the world only through their own eyes. Rachel had more than once tried Sarah's own patience with her rash antics.

"You still will not concede you were wrong?"

Ben hunched his shoulders. "What choice did I have?"

"You put yourself in the situation. No one else."

His brother's petulant expression became more pronounced. "Easy enough for you to say."

Lord Chance gave a slow shake of his head. "No, Ben, it is very difficult for me to say, which is why I have held my tongue for far too long. You are no longer a child. You cannot fribble away your days at the card table and act the buffoon among Society. And you certainly cannot continue your habit of expecting me to rush to your rescue each time you tumble into disaster."

Ben clenched his hands at the reprimand. Sarah had no doubt the young gentleman was unaccustomed to being spoken to in such a blunt fashion.

"You expect me to follow in the footsteps of the Flawless Earl?" he struck back in anger.

Sarah's breath caught as Lord Chance's expression became icy with displeasure. "I expect you to become a man, and to accept the responsibilities that accompany an adult."

"What responsibilities?"

"To begin with, you must learn to live within your income. For another, I wish you to take command of one of the smaller estates."

Ben's eyes widened with shock. "You wish me to leave London?"

Lord Chance shrugged. "For a few months, at least. Once you have proven you can behave in a responsible manner, you will be allowed to return."

The silence was thick with conflict as the two brothers glared at one another.

"Is that a command?" Ben at last gritted.

"If it must be."

Realizing he was no match for his stronger-willed brother, Ben took a deliberate step backward. "Very well. You win, Chance."

"Ben." The lean features abruptly softened with regret. "I do this for you."

"So you say." Turning abruptly on his heel, Ben stormed from the room. Instinctively, Lord Chance moved to follow after his angry sibling before forcing himself to come to a halt.

Barely aware that she was moving, Sarah

crossed to stand beside his taut frame. She knew precisely what he was feeling—frustration, guilt, and the fear that he had just destroyed the always fragile relationship between siblings.

Rubbing a hand over the tense muscles of his neck, Lord Chance glanced down at her upturned countenance. "Did I do right?" he demanded.

Sarah offered him a rueful smile. "You did what you thought best. It is all any of us can do."

He heaved a sigh. "I suppose."

"At least you have the diamonds," she attempted to comfort him.

An unnervingly tender expression softened his features. "Yes. How can I possibly thank you?"

Sarah felt embarrassed beneath his warm regard. "I did very little."

His hand raised to softly brush her cheek, sending her heart galloping at an alarming pace. "You saved my family from an ugly scandal, you ensured my mother's peace of mind, and you retrieved an irreplaceable heirloom. Hardly very little."

Sarah discovered herself lost in the darkness of his eyes. Sweet, tantalizing warmth spread through her body at the thought that she had pleased him. She would do anything to please this man, she thought inanely. Scour London for missing jewels, brave the December winter to ride at his side in the park, even hand over her heart if he would but ask . . .

She abruptly stiffened as she realized the direction of her thoughts. She was a fool. He would never ask for her heart. He would no doubt be horrified if he ever discovered she had been so dim-witted as to allow his flirtations to sway her emotions. And now that the diamonds had been recovered, he would be walking out of her life without once glancing back.

A sharp, tearing pain ripped through her heart as Sarah struggled not to reveal her terrible secret. "I am just relieved they were recovered," she breathed.

"Sarah . . ." He faltered to a halt as if uncertain what he intended to say. Then, drawing in a deep breath, he abruptly dropped his hand. "You deserve a reward."

Reward? Sarah stepped back as if she had been struck. Did he believe she had offered her services with the expectation of a reward? Did he truly believe she was so shallow? Or was he attempting to soften the blow of their parting like she was some poor mistress being given her congé? Either way, the pain in her body was sharpened by his unwelcome offer.

"I asked for no reward," she said in stiff tones.

A faint frown marred his brow. "I could hardly request your help without offering something in return."

Her chin tilted to a proud angle. "You have already been most generous to the school."

"I am not referring to the school," he said with a hint of impatience. He was obviously accustomed to women who were anxious to accept his generosity. "I wish to give something to you."

"There is nothing I need."

"Absurd." His frown deepened. "Every woman is in need of a few luxuries. I could easily provide you with the means to acquire whatever you desire."

She bit back the hysterical urge to laugh. What she desired was the one thing he could never provide. Squaring her shoulders, she met his gaze bravely. "No."

He blinked at the uncompromising word. "Why are you being so stubborn?"

"I do not accept money from gentlemen."

He flinched at her blunt words, his eyes dark with an emotion that Sarah found impossible to determine. "I am not implying I wish you to become a kept woman," he rasped. "I merely feel you have earned a reward."

"And I have said no."

"Why?"

She could hardly confess that her love for him made the mere idea of a reward for her efforts somehow sordid, so instead she blurted out the first thing that came to mind. "Whatever I need, Lord Scott will provide."

She realized her mistake the minute his eyes narrowed with suspicion. Blast. The last thing she desired was Lord Chance questioning her relationship with the older gentleman.

"Lord Scott?"

She futilely attempted to appear nonchalant. "Yes."

The male features hardened with distaste. "You will accept the generosity of Lord Scott, but not myself?"

"He is my . . . friend."

His hands slowly clenched. "Ridiculously enough, I thought I was your friend."

Unable to brave his piercing regard any longer, Sarah turned about, her hand pressing to the ache lodged deep in her stomach.

"How can we be?" she demanded in unsteady tones. "You now possess the diamonds. We shall never see one another again."

She thought she heard a sharp rasp at her low words.

"Is that what you desire?"

Sarah closed her eyes at the fierce urge to turn and throw herself into his arms. What would it serve? He would still be a gentleman far beyond her reach, and she would still be a maiden with too much honor to become his mistress.

Why prolong the pain?

"It is fate," she said in fierce tones. "We live in two separate worlds. Worlds that have nothing in common."

Although she did not hear him move, Sarah could feel the heat of his body as he halted mere inches from her rigid back. She shivered, desperately wishing she could halt her ridiculous reactions to his mere presence. No other gentleman had ever tangled her nerves in such a fashion.

"They did for a time." His husky words tingled down her spine.

"A time that has passed."

"And yet Lord Scott remains a part of your world."

Heavens above, why did he not leave her in peace, she wondered in desperation. He could not desire to continue their strange relationship. Did he feel guilt at walking away and leaving her once again on her own?

The mere thought he might pity her stiffened her resolve. She could not bear the thought of being the object of sympathy. She had survived a good many years without Lord Chance in her life. She would certainly survive when he was gone. "That is different," she said firmly.

"Ah, yes. He is such a dear friend." The mocking bitterness in his tone gave her the strength to turn and stab him with a glittering gaze.

"What do you want from me?"

"I . . ." He halted at the sight of her rigid expression, a nerve twitching in his tightly clenched jaw. "Nothing. Nothing at all."

Sarah drew in a shuddering breath, needing to be away from this man who created such a burning ache in her heart. "Perhaps you would be kind enough to drive me home."

His lips thinned. "Of course."

In brittle silence, they left the town house and entered the waiting carriage. Sarah determinedly stared out the small window as if she had never before beheld the passing houses and the occasional street vendor braving the frigid rain.

Inside the carriage, the air was even more frigid. Sarah could feel his black gaze searing her profile, but she forced herself to maintain her stoic silence. There was nothing left to say.

Nothing but good-bye.

The drive across town seemed to last an eternity, but at last they pulled to a halt. His precise manners too ingrained to ignore, he stiffly escorted her to the door.

As they waited for Watts to make his appearance, Lord Chance cleared his throat. "Thank you, Miss Cresswell, for all you did for my family."

Sarah kept her gaze firmly on the tips of her boots. "You are welcome, my lord."

"I . . . I hope you have a happy Christmas."

She shivered, knowing her Christmas was bound to be as bleak as the weather. "I wish you the same," she muttered. Then, as the door at last opened, she breathed out a shaky sigh. "Good-bye, my lord."

She did not wait to discover if he had anything further to say. Indeed, she practically dashed through the open door and into the foyer. She had to be away from Lord Chance. She did not want him to see the tears already blurring her gaze.

Her flight led her up the stairs and to the landing before she was abruptly halted as her father stepped out of the library.

"There you are, my dear," he pronounced with a pleased smile. "Join me for tea?"

Sarah blinked back her tears with an effort. Dear heavens, all she wanted was the solitude of her room so she could nurse her wounds in private.

Surely that was not so much to ask for.

"No, thank you," she murmured, her head bent to hide her distress.

The Devilish Dandy, however, was far too shrewd to be easily fooled. He swiftly moved to stand at her side. "What has occurred?"

Knowing it would be a wasted effort to attempt to deceive Solomon Cresswell, Sarah reluctantly lifted her pale countenance. "The diamonds have been recovered."

Solomon arched a dark brow. "Indeed?"

"Yes, Mr. Coltran's friend had taken them."

There was a brief pause as her father carefully studied her reddened eyes. "I suppose Lord Chance is pleased?"

"Very pleased."

"And you?" he asked softly.

She lifted her hands in a vague motion. "Relieved that it is at an end."

Her father's lips twisted with wry disbelief. "You look as if you have lost your best friend."

Sarah felt her stomach twist. Her father was precisely right. She had lost her best friend. Beyond the tingling heat he inspired and the pleasurable sensation of being a desirable female, there was the utter delight of simply being in his company—the way he made her laugh, the absolute attention he gave to her every word, and how he had shared with her the man behind the image of the Flawless Earl.

That is what she would miss.

Every single day of her life.

Still, she was not prepared to share such emotions with anyone. Not even her father. "I am quite well," she lied.

Solomon tilted his head to one side. "Will you be seeing Lord Chance again?"

"No." She shook her head, her hands pressed to her stomach. "Why should I?"

"Because you love him."

Sarah gasped as she took an instinctive step backward. Had she been so obvious? "Absurd."

"Sarah." With a swift motion, Solomon removed the satin eye patch to regard her in an uncharacteristically somber fashion. "You cannot fool me. I have seen it in your eyes. You have fallen love with Lord Chance."

Her lips trembled as she battled to maintain her composure. "What would it matter if I had? Nothing could come from such emotions."

He reached out to gently tip her face upward. "Why?"

She reluctantly met his gaze. There were moments when she wondered what life might have been like if her father had been just another gentleman among the *ton*, what it might have been like to be raised free of scandal and with every opportunity to move through Society as any other debutante. But such thoughts were always swiftly dismissed. Whatever his numerous faults, she did love her father, and never for a moment did she doubt his love for her.

"Oh, Father, you of all people should know why," she said with a sad smile.

A grimace of regret marred his thin features. "Because you are my daughter."

Sarah stepped back. The day had been fraught with emotional confrontations. She did not feel capable of facing yet another. "Please forgive me, Father. I must lie down."

She turned toward the stairs that led to her private chambers as her father's voice floated softly through the air. "I am sorry, Sarah. . . ."

Her head bowed in sorrow. "Yes, I know, Father."

Fifteen

The Grecian bowl was exquisite.

Delicately molded, with traces of the original paint still intact, it was one of his best purchases to date. And yet, as he aimlessly sketched the priceless object, Lord Chance was forced to acknowledge it might as well be a lump of clay.

Blast and damnation.

With an exasperated motion, he tossed aside his piece of charcoal.

He had been so determined when he had awakened this morning. It had been two days since he had left Sarah at her home and driven away, two days that he had moped about this blasted house and accomplished little more than emptying a number of brandy bottles. Today he had risen with the resolution to put Miss Cresswell out of his thoughts and return to the life that had always brought him a great deal of satisfaction.

After all, she had made it decidedly clear that their relationship was at an end. She would not even accept a paltry gift for her efforts. And he had known from the beginning his connection would be but a fleeting thing. Even when he had held her in his arms and tasted her sweetness, he had known deep within him his desire was doomed to remain unquenched.

So why could he not reclaim the contentment he had once taken for granted?

He pressed his slender fingers to his temples in an effort to relieve the pain in his head.

At least the diamonds had been returned, he attempted to console himself. It was the day before Christmas, and tonight, when his mother prepared for her grand event, she would have no inkling they had ever been missing. Her only regret would be that her beloved son had taken an odd notion to travel to their estate in Kent.

It was a hollow triumph, he was forced to acknowledge. He had regained the diamonds, but in the process he had lost the most beautiful and gracious woman in the world. Hardly a fair bargain.

The pounding in his head only increased at the thought of his mother's party. Gads, the last thing he desired was to be surrounded by a hundred chattering guests as he attempted to pretend that all was right with the world. And worse would be the endless debutantes with their determined mamas all angling to attract his elusive interest. How could he not compare them to the woman who was so utterly their superior?

He would give his fortune to send his regrets. Surely he could conjure some dread ailment to excuse his presence. But the knowledge that he had already taken Ben from her side halted his desire to cry craven. His mother would never forgive him if he left her in the lurch.

No, duty demanded that he at least make an appearance for the party, as well as attend the

Christmas supper she was sure to have planned for the morrow.

Duty.

Chance grimaced. He was swiftly beginning to despise the very word.

The sound of the library door being pushed open brought his dark thoughts to an abrupt end. The sight of his butler did nothing to ease his sudden tension. The last occasion Pate had intruded upon his privacy he had discovered his brother was a thief. He did not need yet another disaster.

"Pardon me, my lord," Pate murmured.

Chance leaned back in his seat in a weary motion. "What is it, Pate?"

"A Monsieur Valmere to see you."

"Damn," Chance muttered in exasperation. He had spent several hours pondering the mysterious Monsieur Valmere. Although he had come to no firm conclusions, he was certain the man was not who he pretended to be. He also suspected he was more closely related to Sarah than either wished to admit.

What the devil could he want?

Did he desire the reward Sarah had so vehemently refused?

If he were indeed the Devilish Dandy, it would certainly fit his style.

"Shall I tell him you are not at home?"

Chance smiled wryly, wishing he could rid himself of the gentleman so easily. "Do not bother. I have a peculiar notion that if Monsieur Valmere desires to speak with me, there is precious little we can do to halt him."

Pate gave a startled blink. "My lord?"

"Just show him in," Chance commanded with a sigh.

"Very good."

"Oh, and bring my best brandy," he called out as the butler backed through the doorway. "I shall no doubt have need of it."

Rising to his feet, Chance glanced briefly at the pier mirror over the side table. Despite his elegant plum coat and precisely knotted cravat, there was a pallor to his countenance he could not conceal, which was no doubt the reason his servants had been tiptoeing through the house as if there had been a death in the family, he acknowledged wryly. Odd, considering they had been annoyingly jubilant after his rather scandalous tête-à-tête with Miss Cresswell.

With an elegant motion, he adjusted a dark curl, and then turned to regard the decidedly flamboyant gentleman who swept through the door.

"My lord." Monsieur Valmere performed a deep bow.

"Monsieur Valmere."

"So good of you to see me."

Chance raised his brows. "Did I have a choice?"

A hint of a smile touched the thin face. "No."

Just for a moment there was something in that countenance that sharply reminded him of Sarah. He stiffened in pain. Gads, would he ever find peace? "What do you desire?"

The gentleman nonchalantly crossed his arms over the width of his chest. "You surely realize I've come to speak with you of Miss Cresswell."

Absurdly, Chance hadn't. Why should he? Miss

Cresswell had appeared perfectly satisfied to see the last of him.

Then he was suddenly struck with a new, wholly unwelcome thought. "She is well, is she not?" he demanded in sharp tones.

"Non, ma fille is distressingly unwell."

Chance clenched his fists at the ludicrous French accent. "Do not toy with me," he warned, his heart wrenching at the mere thought Sarah might be ill or even injured. "What has occurred?"

"You," Monsieur Valmere said simply.

Chance's brows snapped together. "What?"

"She is in love with you."

Chance sucked in a harsh breath. "Ridiculous."

"That is precisely what I attempted to tell her, but to no avail. She is convinced you are deserving of her heart."

His lips thinned. "I suppose that is why she insisted she never wished to see me again."

Monsieur offered a shrug. "What did you expect? She believes there is no future in such a relationship."

Sarah loved him?

Was it possible?

Against his will, the memory of her innocent response to his kisses flashed through his mind. He had known she was physically attracted to him and that her beautiful eyes seemed to glow a bit brighter when he entered the room.

But love?

A poignant longing rushed through his blood before he was sternly taking command of his foolish weakness.

Knowing Sarah returned his feelings did not

solve their troubles. Indeed, it only made it worse. He could hardly bear the thought she was suffering the same tortures as himself.

"There is no future," he forced himself to say in harsh tones.

Monsieur Valmere calmly removed a snuff box to measure a small pinch. "You do not love her?"

Chance paused before heaving a resigned sigh. "Of course I do."

"And yet you intend to put her out of your life?" He dusted his fingers before returning the gold box to his pocket. "You can so easily turn your back on her?"

Wincing at the callous accusation, Chance took a step forward. "There is nothing easy about it, but I have a duty to my family. I must think of their honor."

"How very noble," the older man mocked, clearly unimpressed with Chance's painful sacrifice. "Pray tell me how a young maiden who devotes her life to others and loves with such generosity could ever bring dishonor to a family."

Chance regarded his guest in a deliberate manner. "She is the daughter of a wanted criminal."

He gave a brief nod of his head at the direct hit before running a finger over the satin eye patch. "What if I promise the Devilish Dandy shall never return and never trouble you?"

"Can you make such a promise?"

Realizing he was as much as admitting he was indeed the wanted criminal, the gentleman gave a slow nod of his head. "Yes."

Chance could not help but admire the man's pluck. One shout from him would no doubt bring a swift end to the Devilish Dandy. And yet he had risked his very neck to bring happiness to his child.

Of course, Chance had no intention of handing the thief over to the proper authorities, not even when Pate entered the room with the decanter of brandy. He would never willingly hurt Sarah in such a fashion.

Waiting for the butler to retire from the room, he poured them both a glass before pacing toward the crackling fire. "All this does not alter the fact that any connection with Miss Cresswell is bound to bring scandal to my family."

"Fah. What is a bit of gossip when compared to a lifetime without the woman you love?"

Chance ground his teeth together. Damn, but the man seemed to know where to strike. "And what of my mother and brother? They will endure the same scandal as I."

"You know, I do not believe you think of your mother or brother at all," the older man slowly accused. "I believe you are merely frightened."

Frowning, Chance turned to confront his unwelcome guest. He did not readily endure being called a coward. Not by anyone. "I beg your pardon?"

Indifferent to the danger carved into Chance's elegant features, the Devilish Dandy met his gaze squarely.

"It is simple to follow the path that is expected of you. It takes far more courage to follow the convictions of your heart." He lifted his hand as Chance opened his mouth to argue. "Sarah possess such courage each day she goes to that school or those brothels where no lady should be seen. It was the same courage her mother possessed when she left her family and faced ruin to wed Solomon Cresswell. She was cut off by everyone but Lord Scott."

Chance pounced upon the familiar name. "Lord Scott?"

"Sarah's uncle. Although few are privy to the relationship," the gentleman shocked Chance by admitting. "It was a sacrifice she made for love."

Chance gave a slow shake of his head, at last realizing why Sarah and Lord Scott appeared to be so close.

Good gads, Sarah was related to one of the most influential families in England, but her place in Society had been taken away by the gentleman standing before him. If only . . . no, he drew his thoughts up sharply. There was no if only. The Devilish Dandy had made certain of that.

"It was a sacrifice she also made for her children," he pointed out in sharp tones.

"Yes. And she would be the last person to regret producing three beautiful daughters who are as kind and sweet natured as they are lovely. Hardly a legacy to be ashamed of."

Chance could not deny the truth in his words. Sarah was lovely and kind natured and blessed with the goodness to change the world.

No mother could regret such a daughter.

"You make it all sound so simple."

The older man gave a slow shake of his head. "No. I have told you it takes the courage of your convictions. It would be simple to remain the Flawless Earl and dutifully take a proper maiden to fill your nurseries. The difficult path is risking all for love."

Chance's heart shuddered to a halt.

To risk all for love . . .

Heavens above, did he dare follow his heart? Did he possess such courage?

His answer came as a pale countenance with a pair of brilliant blue eyes rose to his mind.

Whatever trials they might face, surely they could overcome them together.

Wasn't that what love was for?

"I'm off to the country for a few weeks." The Devilish Dandy intruded upon his whirling thoughts. "I am certain Sarah could use a friend."

With this parting shot, the Devilish Dandy turned to leave the room.

Alone, Chance allowed the first smile in days to curve his lips.

Across town, Sarah was doing her best to conjure up a holiday spirit. It hardly seemed fair to allow her poor disposition to dampen the entire household. Besides which, she could not remain locked in her room for an eternity, she had chastised herself. It would be far better to plunge back into her normal routine and put the past few weeks behind her.

All very sensible notions, she told herself as she placed the last of the holly onto the mantel. Unfortunately, her heart would just not cooperate.

Blinking back the ever ready tears, she turned to regard Lucky with a brisk smile.

"What do you think, Lucky?"

The young lad closely surveyed the room swathed in Christmas greenery. "There ain't no mistletoe," he at last concluded.

Sarah thinned her lips, refusing to contemplate where mistletoe had led her on the last occasion.

Blasted stuff.

"We have no need for such foolishness."

Lucky cast her a sly glance. "What if his lordship comes a-calling?"

Sarah stiffened in spite of herself. "If you are referring to Lord Chance, you needn't raise your hopes, Lucky," she said sternly. "The diamonds have been found, and Lord Chance has no further use for our services."

"I should not be so hasty, Miss Cresswell," a dark voice drawled from the doorway.

Sarah's heart halted as she spun about to discover the all too familiar form of Lord Chance in the center of the room. "My lord."

Unfettered by Sarah's own conflicting emotions at the sight of the gentleman who had become such a vital part of their lives, Lucky let loose a loud whoop. "Cor, I knew you'd be back."

Lord Chance reached out to ruffle the boy's hair with genuine fondness. "I believe if you go to my carriage you will find a trifling gift for you."

"A rare 'un you be, guv." Lucky grinned before darting from the room.

Alone with the man who had haunted her thoughts for the past two days, Sarah struggled to breathe. Dear heavens, she had worked so hard to convince herself it was all for the best that she never clap eyes upon him again. Now he had managed to destroy the illusion by merely stepping into the room. "What are you doing here?" she demanded in shaking tones.

He slowly held up a small package. "I have brought you a Christmas gift."

Sarah instantly rebelled at the soft words. "I

thought I had made it clear that I desire nothing."

His handsome features twisted. "Painfully clear. However, I am as wretchedly stubborn as you and I will not be swayed." Stepping forward, he thrust the gift into her hands. "At least open it."

Unnerved by the heat and male scent that wrapped about her, Sarah found her fingers fumbling with the heavy paper. It was not that she wished for a gift, she told herself sternly, it was simply that she would do whatever necessary to bring this encounter to a swift end.

Expecting a lavish jewel or even a crude bank note, she was caught off guard by the leather-bound collection of Shakespeare's sonnets. It was a gift a gentleman might give an aunt or even his mother, but she discovered her wariness melting to pleasure. "Oh."

His dark gaze never left her wide eyes. "You mentioned you preferred Shakespeare to any other poet."

She gave a startled blink. "And you remembered?"

"I remember . . . everything," he breathed softly. "Every word, every glance, every kiss."

She was being drawn into the dark magic of his eyes, and she desperately grasped for a measure of sanity. "You should not be here."

"No," he agreed with a rueful smile. "My mother will have my head upon a platter for not being at her gathering."

Sarah gasped. "The Christmas party."

"Yes."

"Why are you not there?"

He raised a hand to cup her face. "Because I will not go without you."

A deep shudder shook her body. "What did you say?"

"I love you, Sarah Cresswell."

An icy shock raced through her body, making it nearly impossible to think clearly. He loved her? But it wasn't possible, was it? He was going to marry some impeccable debutante who would bring nothing but honor to the role of countess, not the daughter of a jewel thief who devoted her life to the poor and outcast. "You do not know what you are saying."

"I know precisely what I am saying," he insisted as he placed his other arm about her waist. "I love you. I love how you smile, how your eyes sparkle when you are amused, how you fill the world with happiness, and how you tremble in my arms."

Tears filled her eyes at his gentle words. "But . . . it is impossible."

"The only thing impossible is living my life without you."

She gazed into the dark eyes that seemed to consume her. "What do you want from me?"

His hand moved to stroke the soft fullness of her lips. "I want you to be my wife. Marry me, Sarah."

Her heart cried out to say yes.

It was, after all, what she desired more than anything in the world. But the streak of stubborn logic that was so much a part of her warned it was not nearly so simple.

"Your family will never accept me," she said in husky tones.

His expression never altered. "That is their choice, of course, but I do not doubt they will soon come to love you as much as I do." A wicked glint suddenly burned in his eyes. "Especially when you have graced the Chance nurseries with a variety of heirs."

An embarrassed heat stained her cheeks. "I can bring nothing but scandal."

"No," he denied sternly. "You bring beauty and grace and the most amazing heart."

Those fingers were so devilishly distracting, she thought inanely. They stirred up a dizzying excitement that clouded her mind and made her knees threaten to buckle. More importantly, they made her forget all the sensible reasons she should not become Lady Chance.

"I do not know . . ."

"Tell me one thing, Sarah," he demanded. "Do you love me?"

"Yes, but . . ."

The fingers pressed her lips to silence. "No. Nothing else is important. Share my life with me. Be my wife."

Sarah wavered, caught between fear and the love-burning in his eyes. She had always tried to do what was best for others, to put her own needs and wishes aside. But for once she discovered she could not deny the aching desire to snatch happiness with both hands. For once she would please herself and the devil take the world.

"Oliver," she breathed with a tremulous smile.

He gave a strangled groan before his head swooped downward and he claimed her lips in a heady kiss. Sarah swayed forward, reveling in the unyielding strength of his male frame. Oh, to be held like this for an eternity, she thought dreamily. It was more than any woman could wish for.

Scattering soft kisses over her upturned face,

Oliver at last pulled back to gaze down at her shimmering eyes.

"Lucky was correct," he teased softly. "We do need mistletoe."

Her smile could have rivaled the Christmas star burning brightly overhead. "You seem to be doing quite well without it."

"I must have been overcome with the Christmas spirit," he murmured.

Sarah's eyes abruptly widened. "Oh . . . I did not get you a Christmas gift."

His dark eyes smoldered with a sudden fire. "You are mistaken, my love. You have given me a gift more precious than any other." His head began to lower once again. "The courage to follow my heart. Happy Christmas, my dearest."

"The happiest ever," she sighed as his lips closed over her own.

Neither noticed the Devilish Dandy as he slipped out the door and headed upstairs to pack his trunk.

One daughter had been suitably settled, he acknowledged with a smile. There were two to go before he could comfortably retire to his villa in Italy.

Dearest Emma was next.

He would need to find a most special gentleman, he decided. A gentleman who could thaw her ice and make her laugh again.

Whistling a Christmas carol, he set about his plans.

The Devilish Dandy never failed.

ABOUT THE AUTHOR

Debbie Raleigh lives with her family in Missouri. She is currently working on THE VALENTINE WISH (Emma's story) coming in January, 2002. Debbie loves to hear from readers, and you may write to her c/o Zebra Books. Please include a self-addressed stamped envelope if you wish a response.

More Zebra Regency Romances

__A Taste for Love by Donna Bell $4.99US/$6.50CAN
0-8217-6104-8

__An Unlikely Father by Lynn Collum $4.99US/$6.99CAN
0-8217-6418-7

__An Unexpected Husband by Jo Ann Ferguson $4.99US/$6.99CAN
0-8217-6481-0

__Wedding Ghost by Cindy Holbrook $4.99US/$6.50CAN
0-8217-6217-6

__Lady Diana's Darlings by Kate Huntington $4.99US/$6.99CAN
0-8217-6655-4

__A London Flirtation by Valerie King $4.99US/$6.99CAN
0-8217-6535-3

__Lord Langdon's Tutor by Laura Paquet $4.99US/$6.99CAN
0-8217-6675-9

__Lord Mumford's Minx by Debbie Raleigh $4.99US/$6.99CAN
0-8217-6673-2

__Lady Serena's Surrender by Jeanne Savery $4.99US/$6.99CAN
0-8217-6607-4

__A Dangerous Dalliance by Regina Scott $4.99US/$6.99CAN
0-8217-6609-0

__Lady May's Folly by Donna Simpson $4.99US/$6.99CAN
0-8217-6805-0

Call toll free **1-888-345-BOOK** to order by phone or use this coupon to order by mail.

Name_____

Address_____

City_____ State_____ Zip_____

Please send me the books I have checked above.

I am enclosing $_____

Plus postage and handling* $_____

Sales tax (in New York and Tennessee only) $_____

Total amount enclosed $_____

*Add $2.50 for the first book and $.50 for each additional book.

Send check or money order (no cash or CODs) to:

Kensington Publishing Corp., 850 Third Avenue, New York, NY 10022

Prices and numbers subject to change without notice.

All orders subject to availability.

Check out our website at **www.kensingtonbooks.com**.

Celebrate Romance With One of Today's Hottest Authors

Amanda Scott

Discover The Magic of Romance With
Jo Goodman